FELL FOR THE OPP 2

Dove & Cj's Love Story

AUBRY J.

Fell for the Opp 2

Published by Grand Penz Publications

WANT TO BE A PART OF THE GRAND PENZ FAMILY?

To submit your manuscript to Grand Penz Publications,
please send the first three chapters and synopsis to
grandpenzpublications@gmail.com

SYNOPSIS

Dove Lincoln planned to live her life to the fullest. She had a good job, her man right beside her, and her mother was out of prison. Things were going well... until they weren't. Her past was starting to cause problems in her present. Even though she put a bullet in her ex, Tika, he was still causing problems from the grave. Her ex's best friend Red was back and had a secret that could destroy Dove.

Clever "CJ" Jones would do anything to protect his woman and his business. People knew and respected his name when they heard it. When the police started connecting the dots to old cases, and CJ's name was brought up, he had no other choice but to make a deal with the man he vowed to have nothing to do with. The people around him weren't who he thought they were, and loyalty was being questioned every time he turned around.

These two swore they're in it for the long haul. Now things didn't look too good. Deals are being made, shots are being fired, and love is being tested. Now both CJ and Dove are both questioning whether they made the right decision.

Chapter One

DOVE

"Did you think we would end up like this?" I questioned as I pulled the sheet over my body. I watched as CJ got dressed. He looked up at me and smiled that goofy lopsided smile that he only gave me and winked. No lie, I instantly got wet and had to squeeze my legs together. He put his shirt down at the end of the bed and grabbed my ankle before I could pull away.

"Nah man, come here," CJ said as he pulled me towards him. I did as I was told for two reasons: one, this man had my heart, and I knew he'd never do anything to hurt me, and two, because I was curious about what he would say. He stepped back as I sat on the end of the bed. Like the kid I was at heart, I swung my feet back and forth as I adjusted the sheet around my body once again. "Ask me that question again," he said as he tilted my face up to look at him.

"Did you think we'd end up like this?" I asked him again. I'd never been an insecure woman. I knew, without a doubt, what I brought to the table and my resume spoke for itself. But CJ wasn't the type of man I pictured myself with. He was a street king. People knew his name, respected it, and without a doubt, feared it. I saw how people looked at me now when we are out. Women were envious. Shit, and some men, too. They wanted what was mine but didn't understand how I got it.

"What did I tell you when we started this?" he questioned as he stepped in between my legs. Looking up at him, I watched as the different emotions ran across his face. In the street he was unemotional, and at times, downright cruel. But with me he was gentle, caring, and respectful. "Don't even answer that. You know exactly what I said. What's up with the insecure shit you pulling right now? You know how hard I worked to get you and keep you. So why play the games?"

"I'm not playing games, it was just a question," I replied as I pulled my face from his hands. I found myself catching an attitude and not meaning to, so I had to pull back before I did or said something that would result in us having an argument. "Look, just let it go. What I'm trying to say isn't coming out right, and I don't have the time to go back and forth." I pushed him back slightly so that I could stand. But, because CJ was at times an ass, he didn't move. Instead, he stepped closer to me, making me lean back on my elbows and look up at him. "CJ, please move. I have to get ready for work."

"Give me a kiss," CJ replied with a smirk on his face as he bent down.

Instead of just kissing me, he waited for me to meet him halfway. The second our lips met, every insecurity I had about him, and us, disappeared. He let out a small growl as he deepened the kiss. He pushed his tongue through my lips and into my mouth, fighting for dominance, some type of control over the situation, and he didn't even realize he had it already. I fell completely back on the bed and wrapped my arms around his neck. I could feel his dick harden against me, and even though I was sore from last night, my pussy got wetter at the thought of him being back inside me.

Without breaking our kiss he freed himself from his underwear and pushed inside me. I pulled my face away from him and gasped from the feeling of him inside me. He planted his hands on the bed next to my head and waited for me to adjust to his size. When I nodded my head, he started pulling back, only to push back inside me with so much force I damn near yelled at the top of my lungs. The shit hurt and felt good at the same time.

"Don't ever question what we have or what we are," CJ said with each thrust.

I reached up and wrapped by hands around his wrists as I wrapped my legs around his waist. No lie, at this point this man could've told me anything and I would've agreed to it. The way he fucked me on a regular let me know he wasn't playing with me. I nodded my head as I looked up at him. To keep from crying out, I bit on my bottom lip. It didn't stop the moans, but I refused to give him the satisfaction of only being inside me for a few minutes before he had me telling him everything he wanted to hear. The shit is twisted, I know. I liked the pain and the pleasure of being fucked by a man who was on a mission to prove a point.

"Don't give a damn nod, Dove. Verbally answer me."

Even though he was breathing heavy, I knew for a fact he wasn't close to being done. So instead of answering him like I knew he wanted, I nodded my head again.

"Oh so you think this shit a game, huh?" CJ questioned as he pulled out of me. "Roll your ass over and arch like you're supposed to."

This time, I smirked as I did what I was told. Facing forward, I stretched my arms above my head, with my head down, I arched my back and waited for him to do his thing.

"Listen to me and understand what I am going to say to

you. Because, at this point, I'm not going to repeat myself," CJ said as he smacked my right ass cheek.

I whimpered but didn't say anything. He soothed the sting with a kiss, only to repeat the action on my left side. He stood behind me and caressed my ass. Every so often, he'd kiss a cheek, but for a few minutes, he didn't say a word. Then, he pushed inside me.

"You are my world. Besides my baby, there ain't a soul on this earth that I'd die for. Any and everything in this world that you want is yours. It doesn't matter what it is, because as a man, it's my job to provide for you. Don't come to me with no bullshit about how we got here, or if I ever thought we would. 'Cause I can tell you right now, Dove, you were meant to be mine. From the second I saw you, I knew that, and I'm just waiting on you to realize it so we can move this forward."

He pulled out again and started eating my pussy from the back. The shit felt so good, and with his words on repeat in my head, I rode his face. CJ wasn't about games, and if he said it, he meant it. He sucked, licked, and fucked my pussy and asshole with his tongue, making me cum a few times, before he pushed his dick back inside me. But this time wasn't gentle like before. He was on a mission to prove his point. He grabbed a handful of my braids and pulled my head back, kissing the side of my face as he went to work on my pussy.

"Now, I'm going to ask you again. Do you understand what the fuck I am telling you?" CJ questioned as he pumped into me harder. The only sounds that could be heard through the room were my moaning, and our bodies slapping against each other. "Answer my question, Dove, and I'll let you cum," he grunted out as he adjusted his stance and started to hit my favorite spot, which automatically had my legs starting to shake.

"Yes, CJ. Damn! I understand!" I all but shouted and nodded my head. My head was starting to spin and my body tingled everywhere. Him and his damn dick always put me on a high that rivaled any high I'd ever been on.

"Good, now don't play with me like that again," CJ grunted as he began to move faster. He reached around me and started to play with my clit.

I was seeing double and couldn't form the words to tell him I was cumming again. But it didn't matter, I knew without a doubt he could feel my pussy clenching and releasing him over and over. Even though his movement wasn't sloppy, I knew his nut was creeping up on him, too. My orgasm hit me so hard I almost passed out, which was something that happened often as hell since I'd been dealing with CJ.

I stood in the shower, not even twenty minutes later, attempting to wash myself but I couldn't stop the tears that fell from my eyes. I don't know about y'all, but it's something about a man declaring his love for me that made me want to cry. And each time CJ did that shit, I broke down. There wasn't a doubt in my mind that he meant every word he'd said to me. He made sure to show and prove it daily. I put my face under the water to wash away my tears. The last thing I wanted was for him to see me and think something was wrong.

"I left your smoothie in the fridge. Make sure you grab it on your way out," CJ said with a knock on the shower door. Because I never closed the bathroom door when I showered, I turned my face from the water and watched him through the clear door. He stood there looking at his phone, dressed in a pair of black slacks, an orange button up long-sleeved shirt, black vest, and a pair of black loafers. His beard and hair had been cut last night, so his lineup was perfect. "You hear me, Dove?" he questioned without looking up.

"Yes, I heard you," I responded with a laugh. At the sound of my voice, he took his eyes off his phone and looked up at me. He smirked as he shook his head. His eyes watched the movement of my hands as I rubbed the loofa against my skin. He had no shame as he allowed his eyes to scan my entire body before making eye contact with me. "And I thank you."

"You're welcome, baby," he said with a smirk on his face as he adjusted his growing dick through the front of his pants. He knew I wasn't just thanking him for the food, or the sex we'd had a little while ago or last night. I was thanking him for everything. Thanking him for being him and thanking the man upstairs for putting him in my life.

"I love you, Clever," I said to his back as he left the room and I shut off the water. I hung up my loofa, pulled my towel down, and opened the shower door. Wiping my feet on the floor mat, I mentally went over my checklist in my head of things I needed to do when I got off work. I dried off, put lotion on, and got dressed in under thirty minutes. Grabbing my smoothie, I made my way out the door ahead of schedule.

What I didn't expect to see when I opened up the garage, was my oldest brother Memphis sitting on the hood of his car, smoking a black. I shut off my car but didn't get out. Memphis and I hadn't spoken in almost ten years. His mama didn't like the fact that she was a side piece and kept him away from us, after my mama whooped her ass for what seemed like the millionth time. Even though our mama told us to stay away from him, I didn't listen. My brother was my world, so I would sneak around and hang out with him. Memphis was about three years older than Falcon, but was heavy into the streets, even at a young age. People knew his name, knew how he got down, and that he wasn't afraid of a damn soul, and that included my mama.

"Get out the car, Dove. We got some shit to talk about," Memphis said as he released the smoke from his mouth and dropped his foot from the front bumper. He looked exactly like our father, tall, dark, and muscular, long face, thick lips, pointed nose, and thick eyebrows. He had a five o'clock shadow and a pair of piercing green eyes. His hair wasn't cut, but his lineup was sharp, so more than likely he was growing his hair out.

I swallowed a lump in my throat I didn't realize I had as I nodded my head. With shaking hands, I opened the door. I rubbed my stomach thinking of the child that was growing inside of me that CJ knew nothing about.

Shit was about to hit the fan.

Chapter Two

CJ

"Benny, this is a good investment. The money is flowing, and the people know this is the spot to be to record their music. Producers, rappers, singers, shit even DJ's come through that bitch, making hit after hit," Mickey said adjusting his tie as he stood from his desk. He pushed his chair out the way, reached for a few folders, and handed them to us. I didn't need to open it to know it held the numbers that he was talking about. I'd done my research and watched how people moved through the building. It was a good look for us. We'd been discussing moving forward with going more legit, and this was a perfect move for us.

"Yeah, I know all that," Benny mumbled as he looked through the folder. His head nodded every few seconds as he read. He grunted at a figure but didn't say anything. He leaned back in his seat, closing the folder, and tapping it against his leg.

"If you know the figures, then what's the problem?" I questioned as I opened the water that had been handed to me when we'd gotten here almost thirty minutes ago.

I wasn't usually one to rush, but I had a funny feeling something was going on. I just couldn't figure out what it was. I knew Dove had left the house and was at work because my location app sent me the notification letting me know where she was. And my grandmother was sitting with Tiny at the hospital while she was doing her physical therapy.

Trigga called me a few weeks ago asking me if there was anyone I trusted to sit with his cousin, and the only person I could think of, besides Dove, was Clever Jones. As soon as I called her and asked if she'd be down for it, she started in on a rant telling me how she was ready for some great grandkids, and since Dove and I were taking too long to give her some then she would adopt some of our friends' kids. When I told her the link that Dove had to the little girl, she was rushing me to give her Trigga's number so she could speak to him herself. She looked at Dove like a grandchild, and if Dove loved Tiny as much as she did, then there was no way she was going to let Tiny be by herself at any given moment. Plus, it gave me an excuse to know where she was at all times. Since the shooting last year, I'd put a few eyes on her. But she ran them off, telling them, and me, that if the Lord was going to call her home, it didn't matter who I put in front of her to stop it, she was going to go.

"Ain't really a problem. I just have my hands in a lot of different investments, and I don't want to raise any red flags with something new. If this can go down without a problem, then yes, I'm all for it. But if too many people have eyes on this place and want in, then I don't want to," Benny said with a shake of his head.

His points were valid. The less people knew about our involvement, the better, because our other businesses were starting to pop up on the radar of a few different cops that I didn't have on my pay roll. Luckily, Stone always gave us a heads-up and we were able to smooth shit over. But I didn't want to look over my shoulder for the rest of my life. My legit business had to be clean, and stay clean, in order for me to keep making money. I couldn't keep lining people's pockets in order to stay ahead of the game. Eventually, I would be losing money instead of making it.

"This deal hasn't even hit the market yet. I know the owner and she's ready to step away from the music game completely. She's selling pretty much everything, and because I know y'all and know y'all about y'all business, I thought of y'all first. I can always go to Aries and tell her to make it known publicly, and I bet before she can finish her sentence at least thirty niggas will be knocking down her door to try and get their hands on it," Mickey said with a shrug of his shoulders and as he dropped back down in his chair. He was right. Shit like this wasn't something that dropped in our laps daily. If Mickey said it was a good idea and could use our legit businesses to give us enough clean money to make this purchase, I would go ahead without Benny.

"Why she stepping away if the money so good?" Benny questioned as he opened the folder again and started looking through it.

Aries had contracts with producers, A&R, and a few labels to rent out her booths exclusively for the next three years. She'd pulled in close to two million a year from those contracts alone. Her rates were right, but niggas had no problem paying the money she asked because they knew her rooms and equipment were always up-to-date and well taken care of.

"Didn't ask her when we had lunch yesterday," Mickey said as he shook his head. "That girl has done whatever since I've known her. If the shit doesn't sit right with her no more, or she gets bored, then she walks away. She makes millions on her other shit."

"Falcon know you having lunch with another female?" I questioned with a laugh as I adjusted my sleeve. I heard Benny suck his teeth in irritation at the mention of Falcon. I threw a curious glance at him but didn't say anything.

Mickey smirked at me, but didn't take his eyes off Benny. He'd heard the noise, too. Sitting up, he propped his elbows on the desk and rested his face in his hands. People liked to try Mickey to see if he was really about that life, but I knew him well enough to know he didn't play about two things: his money and his woman. If you caused problems with either of them, then it wasn't Falcon that people feared, it was him. "Yo Benny, if you got something you need to get off your chest when it comes to my wife, then let me know now."

"Yo wife meddling in my business when it comes to Lily," Benny said raising up in his seat to look Mickey directly in the eye.

I let out a laugh and sat back in my seat. Benny had shit completely wrong. Falcon was the last woman to get into another woman's business, it didn't matter if it was her sister's. I'd heard Dove talking to Lily on the phone the other day, the shit they were going through ain't have shit to do with Falcon. If anything, she was the one playing peace maker and pushing Lily to talk to Benny, instead of just breaking up with the nigga like she wanted to.

"Benny," I said as I reached over and hit his arm to get his attention. I laughed again at the cold look he gave me when he looked over at me. Fool was really in his feelings about some shit he did and ain't even realize it. But Dove and her sisters weren't the type that chased niggas. If you weren't acting right, then they let your ass go. It was the reason a nigga like Bleus was sitting on the sidelines with the title of bestie, even though he acted like Sage's nigga and claimed a kid that wasn't even his. "Nigga, Falcon is on yo' side. That shit don't have nothing to do with her."

"How you know?" Benny questioned as he looked over at me. He looked desperate as hell for information. He wanted to fix the bullshit problems he was having with Lily, but didn't know how. "'Cause the last time she and I talked, she said she was going to hang out with Falcon and figure some shit out. That was nearly three days ago. I've called, texted, and emailed her. Hell, I even booked an appointment for Thursday under a fake name and put down a deposit to get my damn nails done just so I can see her."

"Nigga, you are desperate as hell!" I said as I tried to control my laughter. This nigga was pulling out all the stops just to get his woman's attention.

"Hell yeah I am!" Benny said with a shrug of his shoulders as he sat back in his chair. "Y'all niggas can front if y'all want, but we all know the truth. If either of y'all women just stopped talking to y'all out the blue, just not a fucking word..."

Benny looked confused as hell. Just sitting there like a nigga stuck on the hardest test of his life, but didn't study 'cause he was too cocky to think he didn't have all the answers. Knowing him, he was more upset at himself than he was with Sage, because we grew up with the same mind-set, you never let your woman question herself when it comes to y'all's relationship. Weak niggas thought having a woman be secure in y'all's relationship was only for simps. They'd rather follow behind dumb niggas like Future, instead of men like Russell Wilson, not realizing niggas like Russell had the shit on lock, and niggas like Future were just trying to catch up.

"You trying to say y'all wouldn't fix that shit by any means necessary?"

"Nigga, Dove wouldn't do that shit to me," I said with a shrug. I wasn't being cocky, it was just a fact. I let my woman know how I felt every chance I got, I showered her with love and listened to her verbal and nonverbal cues. If Dove thought it, then I knew about it. It was that damn simple.

"And Falcon would shoot me before she just stopped talking to me," Mickey said. He wasn't lying, either. Falcon was not the one to play games with. She didn't do the fake and phony shit. If she had a problem, then she'd let you know upfront. Now how you decided to handle that was on you. Because once she said her piece, you'd be better off talking to a brick wall than have her listen to your bullshit.

"Since you niggas know so much about what's going on, then tell me what the problem is," Benny huffed as he looked between the two of us. I didn't say anything, just shook my head and opened the second folder Mickey had handed to us. This nigga wanted an easy out because he wasn't used to doing the work when it came to keeping a woman. I wasn't about to make things easy 'cause he was being lazy. It didn't matter if he was my homie or not. Eventually, he gotta grow his ass up.

"Ummm excuse me sir, there are some police here to see you," Mickey's assistant said as she barged into his office.

I turned in my seat and watched as she quickly shut the door behind her and made her way towards us. Her eyes bounced from each of us before they finally stopped at Mickey, who looked bored out his mind at the mention of police in his building.

"Do they have an appointment?" he questioned as she began to put his papers away. Mickey knew better than anyone to never keep important paperwork out in the open if the police around. He'd watched his mentor make that mistake when he was fresh out of college. The police had come to pay him a visit, and he'd gotten cocky and left everything out in the open. Well, the cop that was there saw some papers that involved the person whose death they were investigating. It took them less than twenty-four hours to come back with a warrant to search his office, and then later arrested him for so many crimes he was in federal prison for life, plus some.

"They aren't here for you," Shelly said with a shake of her head as she closed the filing cabinet and turned to face us. "They're here for him."

Chapter Three

DOVE

"Calm your ass down, I can't understand what you are talking about," Falcon said as she put the car in drive and pulled away from my job. I'd been calling her all day, but because Falcon never moved unless she wanted to, it took her nearly five hours to call me back and another two to show up to my job. I'd spent most of the day worried and pacing the floor, because I knew once Memphis left my house, it was only a matter of time before he contacted one of my other sisters, and I didn't know how they would react to the news.

"Falcon, I haven't even said anything," I said with a huff as I rolled my eyes and tried to get comfortable in my seat. She drove a small ass Corvette, and for the life of me, I couldn't figure out why. The damn thing felt so cramped and stuffy.

"You're thinking it, and every time you have a lot of your mind, you have a habit of fidgeting and nitpicking over small stuff to take your mind off of it," Falcon said as she adjusted the temp in the car. She glanced over at me when I didn't say anything and let out a small laugh. She knew she was right, but I refused to acknowledge it. "You may as well tell me what's wrong before we head to see mommy tomorrow. If she sees you're upset, she's going to spend the entire visit trying to figure out what's wrong and how to fix it."

"Ughh," I groaned as I rubbed my hands up and down my face, and without even trying to stop it, my leg began to bounce up and down. I'd completely forgot about going to see our mama tomorrow. I dropped back in my seat and it took everything in me not to cry. Falcon tapped my bouncing leg to get me to calm down. "Look, I can't go see mommy with you tomorrow. I know I said I would, but I can't. Something came up and it's going to take everything in me to stop the bullshit from hitting the fan."

"What kind of bullshit?" Falcon questioned with a raised brow as she looked over at me before pulling her attention back on the road. Big sis was not about to be happy with the news I'd received this morning, but I didn't have any other choice but to tell her.

"Memphis came and saw me this morning," I damn near mumbled. I quickly grabbed the door to brace myself as Falcon swerved through traffic to pull over. People yelled out their windows and blew their horns at us, but she didn't care. Falcon pulled into the driveway of an abandoned house, turning off the car she gave me her full attention.

"Exactly what do you mean Memphis came and saw you today?" Falcon questioned with a raised eyebrow, which was the only indication that she was upset. The rest of her face was blank, but I could see her chest rising and falling quickly.

"When I was leaving for work, he was sitting in the driveway waiting for me," I said to her quickly. I knew a lot of people wanted to say they didn't fear their siblings, especially once they were adults, and that was true for me. I didn't fear Falcon, she'd never hurt me. If anything, she would rather hurt herself first. But I did fear her going after any and everyone who she thought was a threat to any of us.

"What did he say?" Falcon asked as she grabbed her

ringing phone. She sent whoever it was the voicemail without looking at the screen. Just as soon as she sat the phone down it started to ring again. Letting out a sigh she shook her head. Again, her phone rang, but she didn't take her eyes off me. "Dove, what did he say?"

"That Mister popped his head up out the sand and sent a message through a connect that he was on his way back here because he heard mommy is getting out in a few," I said in one breath, intentionally leaving out the part about him saying that eventually he planned to put a bullet in Mickey because of some shit that happen years ago when they ran the streets together. She didn't need to know that part, at least not yet. It'd been over twelve years since their beef had started, and because of Falcon they'd agreed to let things go. But it seemed like Memphis had changed his mind.

"Mister decided to show his face because of mommy. Nah, something ain't adding up," Falcon said as she shook her head. "That nigga been watching her all this time, making sure she didn't open her mouth like he did, and everybody knows she didn't. She only getting out because this nigga never said it was her. He kept referring to his wife."

I nodded my head and watched as she worked through every situation in her head. Falcon turned around and watched as cars passed us, drumming her hands on the steering wheel. Again, her phone started to ring, and just like before, she ignored it.

"I know you said you don't want to see mommy, but I think it would be best if you did. Something is telling me that Mister's old ass is up to something, and the last thing I want is for any of us to be blindsided by his shit," Falcon said without looking over at me. She started her car and pulled off, her phone still ringing, and she continued to ignore it. "If Memphis is here, then that means that Dallas will eventually pop his ass up, too. Them niggas stay running behind each other, and if they are, I got a bullet with each of their names written on it." Falcon nodded her head and pushed her car through traffic. Something told me that even though I was in the car with her Falcon wasn't talking to me, more so just thinking out loud. "We've been through enough shit, watched our mama do a bid for a nigga who couldn't keep his dick in his pants and his hands to himself. Now his no-good ass sons are sniffing around. Nah, shit don't sound right. I'm already dealing with Mickey and his fucking mood swings. The last thing I need to add to my plate is another body 'cause niggas don't know their place."

"Where are we going, Falcon?" I questioned as she turned off the highway. I knew a lot of her hangouts, but this wasn't the way to any of them. She didn't answer me, instead turned up the volume on the radio.

After about twenty minutes, we pulled into a neighborhood near the outskirts of town. You couldn't even see the houses from the street, so I knew without a doubt that this area was expensive as hell. We pulled into a driveway and Falcon pressed a code into the gate. The doors opened slowly. Once they were open, we pulled in, and just like I thought the house was so damn big. I knew whoever owned it was sitting on some money.

"This is a friend of mine's house. Don't worry, he's cool people," Falcon said as she put the car in park and turned it off.

The house was all brick with white shutters. It reminded me of the houses you saw on HGTV with the long widows, wraparound porches, perfect curb appeal and lawns. I followed her lead, got out the car, and almost sat right back down and closed the door. I took a deep breath and prayed to the Lord above as I watched a tall dark-skinned man stand in the doorway. The man standing there was the scariest looking man I'd ever seen my life.

As we made our way to the door, I counted backwards in my head, trying to control myself. His eyes never left Falcon. It was like he was memorized by her and the way she carried herself. He licked his lips slowly and smirked as she made her way up the stairs, crossing his arms over his chest as he leaned against the doorframe. The thing was none of his actions seemed sexual. If anything, he seemed to just appreciate Falcon. His eyes held a large amount of respect for her, he saw her as his equal.

"I thought my security gate malfunctioned when it alerted me that you were out here," the tall man said with a smile on his face once we made it to the top step. "What do I owe the pleasure of this visit, Falcon?"

"I have some questions that I need answered and it seems like you're the only one who can, or better yet will, answer them," Falcon said as she pulled her phone out her pocket. She rolled her eyes and declined the call, stuffing the phone back in her pocket and bringing her attention back to the man. Whoever was calling her wasn't going to stop until she answered and from the looks of it, she had no plans on doing that. "Hamel, this is my sister Dove. Dove, this is Hamel."

"It's nice to meet you, Dove," Hamel said as he put his hand out for me to shake. I looked from my sister to this man, trying to figure out who he was and why we went to him for answers. We quickly shook hands and Hamel brought his attention back to my sister, who nodded her head. "Now, let's get down to business."

Chapter Four

CJ

"Man, get the fuck out of here with this shit. Ain't no way my prints are on no damn gun y'all pulled from the lake out south," I said as I sat back in my seat. I'd been at the police station for nearly six hours. They kept coming with bullshit, but this one was a new one. If I wasn't so careful about the guns I used, I would be sweating bullets right now. I knew, without a doubt, that the gun they were sliding my way in the evidence bag wasn't mine. "If y'all ain't gonna charge me with something, y'all gonna have to let me go."

"See, it's people like you that get so cocky and think we don't have nothing on you when we really do," Detective Holmes said as he put a piece of gum in his mouth.

Me and this beady-eyed fuck ass nigga had history that ran back years. Shit started when we were kids and went to school together. While he was sitting his dorky ass in every AP class offered at our school, I was fucking his sister in the back of the building. When the shit came out, he tried to come at me as a man and tell me to respect his sister, and even though I respected the nigga's heart, I still had to drop his ass for coming at me. I didn't beat his ass too bad, just knocked out his front tooth and blacked both his eyes. But from that day on, that nigga had it out for me. I can't really say I blamed him for it, but the shit was nearly twelve years ago. Eventually, I knew it would come back and bite me in the ass. Especially when I realized who the nigga was when I was down here bailing one of my cousins out of jail a few weeks ago.

"It's not cocky, Detective Holmes. I know for a fact that gun ain't mine," I said looking down at the gun then back up at him. I smirked before I sat back in my seat and crossed my arms over my chest. "If you had anything, you would've showed your hand by now, I been down here what?" I uncrossed my arms and looked at my watch. "Six hours, I been sitting down here listening to you talk about shit that don't have nothing to do with me and I was a good sport. This shit is starting to get on my nerves, and I gotta be home in a few to spend time with my old lady. So like I said earlier, charge me with something or let me go."

"Oh, you mean Dove Lincoln?" Detective Holmes asked with a smirk of his own. He pushed away from the table and shook his head, copying the way I sat in my chair. The fact that he knew my woman's name didn't sit right with me. I didn't let it show. This fool wasn't about to have me in here worried about some shit when I knew, without a doubt, Dove was a rider. "Oh yeah, you are talking about her, huh? What if I said she's the reason you're down here?"

"Then I'd know you were lying, 'cause Dove don't have shit to do with any gun," I said with a shake of my head, even though my mind was racing with how this gun or any gun could be connected to her. Immediately, my mind went back to the night of her graduation. She'd killed Tika in that warehouse. But it was with Falcon's gun, and if anyone was more careful than I was, it was Falcon and Mickey. Falcon had more bodies on her than I did, and Mickey had more on him than she did. If they hadn't been caught by now, then I was for damn sure there wasn't no way that shit was linked to Dove.

"Word on the street is that her ex Tika Smith is missing and has been for almost a year," Holmes said as he shrugged his shoulders.

The interrogation room door opened and in walked another nigga I couldn't stand but was glad he was on my payroll. Mark Peters strolled in. Instead of saying anything, he stood against the closed door. Mark was another funny nigga. On the outside he acted like he was disgusted by the street life. He let the people around him think he thought that because he wore slacks, a badge around his neck, and a gun on his hip, he was better than everyone else. When in all actuality, Mark was a dirty as they got. He not only worked for me, but my homeboy as well. He kept his eyes on everything and everyone, no one knew he worked for us, and we liked it that way.

He let us know when the other cops on our payroll were running their mouths, or taking off the top before coming to us. We'd met him through Mickey. They were half-brothers, same daddy but different mamas. And because they daddy was a deadbeat that didn't claim any of his kids, and Mark grew up in another state, no one knew of the connection. Plus, he was mixed. Wasn't no damn body putting his high yellow damn near white looking ass next to Mickey. Which was a plus for us.

"From what Mark has picked through chatter, it looks like you and Tika had a few words over Dove. Some people even said you threatened to kill him and his people if he came near Dove again," Holmes said. Nigga was mad giddy about it, like he'd just heard the best news in the world and was waiting on someone to confirm it. His little beady ass eyes kept jumping from me to Mark like he had just thrown down the biggest surprise of them all.

"And we all know how bad your temper is CJ," Mark said from his spot. I didn't even acknowledge that nigga. If he let that shit with Tika come out, then it was a reason for it. What I didn't fuck with was the fact he hadn't give me a heads-up, but we could discuss that later.

"We all got tempers, don't we? Last I heard you'd just came back from suspension 'cause you snatched a little boy up that was innocent," I said, looking at Holmes who looked like he wanted to jump across the table, but he knew better. I smiled a little when I watched his stupid ass smile drop from his face. Nigga would eventually learn he wasn't going to win against me. He was lucky I wasn't single, or I'd call his sister up and have her suck my dick just for him to find out. "And Peters, how many times have you tried to arrest me 'cause you didn't like how I looked at you? Like, come on my guy, we all real in this room when it comes to our tempers. Shit, if anything, y'all should be the ones on the other side of this table being questioned, not me."

A quick knock on the two-way glass let me know I was onto something. Peters and Holmes looked at each other but didn't say anything. I shrugged my shoulders and waited. If they wanted to keep talking, I would let them. But I wasn't going to say another word to either of them.

"Look CJ, just let me know what's up, okay?' Holmes said after a few minutes of quiet.

I studied him for a second, he looked stressed. Like if he didn't get something from this interview, he would have to explain to the people higher up on the food chain and he didn't want to do that. That whole tough guy persona was quickly falling apart. Weak ass niggas. "We know—"

Another knock, but this one coming from the door, interrupted Holmes. Peters stepped out the way just as the door opened. In walked my lawyer, Silas Remington. I let a small laugh when I saw Holmes and Peters roll their eyes. Silas didn't even acknowledge them as she sat her briefcase on the table and sat down next to me.

Silas and I went back. She was the youngest sister of a friend, but she acted like she was the oldest. At first glance, Silas looked innocent and almost naïve to the world, but that was the furthest thing from the truth. In all actuality, Silas was raised by a few of the OG's in the drug game. She spent so much time counting stacks of money as a kid that they called her their accountant. Her brothers made names for themselves: one was a producer, and the other owned a few small businesses. But both still had their hands in the drug game, and so did Silas, until she went off to law school. Now she helped the same people stay out of jail that had taken her and her brothers under their wings and raised them.

"Come on now, Silas. What are you doing here?" Holmes questioned as he got up from his seat and went to stand next to Peters.

I watched as Peters didn't say anything, just watched Silas with a look of aggravation and a little lust in his eyes. I glanced over at Silas and watched as she smiled brightly at them, but still didn't say a word. Her green eyes sparkled with humor as she looked between the two of them. If anyone thought this situation was funny, it was Silas. She'd told me a few weeks ago that Peters had asked her on a date, and she turned him down, telling him her big brothers Shiloh and Sterling said they would put a bullet in any of his workers if they tried it with her. From what I heard, Shiloh had come to Peters' house, dragged him in the backyard, and threatened to beat him to death.

What surprised me out of everything, was that Peters didn't back down. He'd told them that he would fight they asses, and then after it was over, he'd ask Silas out again. Silas wouldn't admit it to them, but I'd heard her talking to Dove about it, and she admitted she liked Peters and him standing up to her brothers only added to his appeal. When Dove had asked Silas why she just didn't stick up for him, Silas let her know that if anyone needed help with defending themselves against her brothers, then they weren't for her. So instead of jumping in, she and Shiloh's wife Hunter stood on the back porch and watched them fight. Peters fought both of her brothers, then afterwards asked her out on another date that she turned down. Whole family was crazy as hell, but they were my people.

"Silas?" Peters said as he wiped his hands down his face. This nigga was so stuck on her that even the ass whooping her brothers put on him didn't matter. I nodded my head a little, respecting the fact that he didn't let them put the fear of God in him.

"Yes?" Silas answered with a raised brow as she looked Peters directly in the face. No matter how innocent she looked, everyone that Silas was not one to fuck with.

"You gonna tell us why you're here?" Peters said as he stuffed his hands into his pocket. I could tell from the way he was moving he didn't know what to do with himself. Silas was playing a damn mind game with this man and didn't even try to act like she wasn't.

"Oh yeah, I'm just waiting on you to formally charge my client with something," Silas said in her quiet, soothing voice that she used when she's getting ready to go in for the kill.

"Silas, your client was brought in for questioning because he was linked to the disappearance of a man," Peters said.

"Again, I am asking if my client is being charged. If not, then we are leaving," Silas said. She smiled brightly at both Peters and Holmes and waited for them to answer her question. "From what I have been told, he hasn't been formally charged. In fact, you brought him in because a CI said he saw him arguing with the missing man over a year ago. If you were so interested in his disappearance, then why didn't you bring him in at that time?"

"How do you know about my CI?" Holmes questioned with a huff. Nigga looked like he wanted to punch a wall because he was so angry. I knew from the past that cops hated for their CI's names to be leaked, 'cause then their information dried up. Holmes began to say something but stopped. He threw his hands up in frustration and walked out the room. Silas let out a soft laugh and shrugged her shoulders as she got up from her seat.

"Well, this was fun and all, but if no charges are being officially being brought up I will take my client and leave," Silas said as we made our way out the door.

We stopped to check out and grab my things from the front desk. Even though I hadn't been charged, they had requested I leave my phone and any other personal items at the front. I did so because I knew they were on some bullshit, and that Mickey and Benny would get in contact with Silas to let her know I was here. I was a lot of things, but a dummy wasn't one. I could see a setup coming a mile away, and these cops were trying to pin my ass to something.

I knew better than to say anything as we walked out the jail. The only sound coming either of us was our shoes clicking against the tile floor. Once we made it to Silas's car, she unlocked it and we got in. Again, no words being said, but this time for two reasons: one, Silas had a rule of never speaking in or near a police station, and two, we both had a million thoughts running through our heads.

"I think they have something, but it wasn't what they brought you in for," Silas as she started her truck. The all-black 2021 Chevy Trailblazer was a birthday gift from her brothers. I couldn't front, it was nice to look at and rode smooth, but it wasn't the luxury I was used to. Crazy thing was, the car fit Silas, though. She didn't see the point of trying to impress anyone. Being a lawyer didn't change that about her, especially since she'd been raised around money. She just liked what she liked and didn't care what other people thought. "What exactly they have, I'm not sure yet. I'm going to pull some strings and see if I can find out anything."

"They had a gun," I said as I adjusted into the seat. I wasn't used to wearing a suit, so the tighter fit of the clothes fucked with me. I was a simple nigga who liked what I liked, and even though suits were starting to grow on me, I wasn't there with always liking how they felt.

"Is it the one that Dove killed Tika with?" Silas questioned. She quickly glanced over at me with a raised brow before turning her attention back to the road. I didn't hide too much shit from Silas, didn't really see the point because she was going to end up finding out everything anyway. Especially if it was something I couldn't hide on my own and needed some extra help.

"Man, you already know it ain't," I said shaking my head. "Falcon made sure that shit was taken care of herself. Whatever they got on me don't have shit to do with Dove no way."

"How can you be so sure?" Silas questioned as she stopped at a red light. With one hand she reached down and pulled her heels off. I let out a laugh as she threw them in her back seat, Silas hated heels more than any other woman I knew. She only wore them for work. Any other time she had on a pair of Nike slides, no matter if she was at home or the office.

"'Cause they mentioned her to see if they could get me to say something," I responded as I pulled my personal phone from my pocket. I wasn't worried about my work one right now, I'd left that at Mickey's office with Benny. I wasn't about to take that bitch into the police station and they mysteriously lose it 'cause they thought I was dumb enough to bring that bitch in there and get caught. Powering it on, I waited for the texts to come through. Benny letting me know that Silas was on her way was the last one I saw before I'd shut it off earlier. My family was solid, they knew not to text me anything while I was there.

"Yeah, they wouldn't have brought her up," Silas said. She drummed against the steering wheel and waited. Every so often, she would glance over at me, but for the most part she just let the music flow through the speakers as she drove me back to my car.

"You know you could just work your magic and have Mark tell you what you need to know," I said with a laugh as we pulled into Mickey's office parking lot.

"I could, but I want to work on some stuff first," Silas said with a roll of her eyes as she put her car in park next to my Benz. I knew she wouldn't outright admit that she was feeling Mark as well, but I could tell she was. Silas didn't open up to many people, but since I'd pretty much grown-up with her people, I knew how she worked. "Whatever they think they have, I can make go away before they even realize it."

"I appreciate it," I said as I opened the door and got out.

I made my way towards my car and got inside. I threw a quick nod to Silas as she honked her horn and pulled off. I didn't live my life being scare of going to jail, I knew better than to think I could always live the type of life I did and not think I would eventually get caught. I just wanted time to get out. I'd spent so much of my time dealing and moving that the legit life didn't look too bad. Especially since Dove had become such an important part of my life. She made things like marriage and kids seem like they weren't too much of a difficult choice. I had faith with Silas on my side. She worked hard to keep her people safe and if she said she was going to work her magic, then I didn't have too much to worry about.

At least, I hoped I didn't.

Chapter Five

DOVE

"Baby, wait a minute," I said as I pushed my braids out of my face and sat down on the edge of the bed.

I'd spent most of the day on my feet and they were killing me. Since I hadn't told CJ I was pregnant, I needed to act as normal as possible. I knew if I started to complain about something as simple as a long day at work, he would know something was off. Not only was my body hurting, but my mind was racing a mile a minute because I'd been waiting on my sisters to call me and let me know how the visit with my mama's lawyer went. We'd gone to visit her last week after visiting with Falcon's friend. The rumors were true. Rose Lincoln was making her way out of jail within the next forty-eight hours.

"I need you to slow down. You're repeating stuff we already knew."

"Okay, okay, yeah you're right, I need to slow it down some," CJ said excitedly as he paced in front of me. Taking a deep breath, he tried to get himself together, but I could tell how excited he was. "So, we already knew that he was working with them. That's how he got your mama to do that bid. But it looks like he been working with them even after that," CJ said. He couldn't stop moving, his arms were going up and down and he couldn't keep the smile off his face. He looked like a little kid was about to burst at the seams if he didn't get whatever it was off his chest.

"CJ, you're making me dizzy with all the moving you're doing," I said to him. I immediately regretted it when he stopped moving and stared at me. His eyes dropped down from my eyes to my stomach then back up. He raised an eyebrow in question but didn't say anything. "Go change your clothes and get yourself together." I had to change the subject back to my father before he let his mind wander. CJ knew my body like the back of his hand, so if he started putting dates and times together, he would realize that I was late, and I didn't need that.

"Right," CJ said with a side glance as he walked into the closet. "So anyway, yo' pops been running his mouth for what looks like a few years before that shit went down with your mama."

"Baby, we already know that much," I said. I could hear him fumbling around in the closet, but I made no effect to move and help him. I'd spent last weekend cleaning up and organizing it, so if he was going to mess it up, I didn't want to see him do it.

"I know," CJ said as he stepped out the closet in a pair of red basketball shorts and a wife beater. "But remember when you said a few weeks ago that your mama was getting out 'cause of some simple ass mistake they didn't check out?"

"Yeah," I replied with a head nod. The whole thing with my mama getting out was still making my head go crazy. My parents were never legally married because my mama never signed the marriage license. After her trial, our mama let her lawyer know that she was not legally his wife and she'd recently found out he was married to another woman. This small detail took nearly three years to verify, because mama's first lawyer died in a car accident a few weeks after her trial. Once we got a new lawyer on it, with the help of CJ, we'd finally started to make progress.

"So, Silas pulled some strings, got a few cops to talk, and slide her some of their files," CJ said as he pulled a pair of Nike Slides from under his side of the bed. "And it looks like that nigga was working with Tika."

"Working with him how, CJ?" I questioned.

"Tika was moving up in the drug game, right?" CJ questioned as he dropped down on the bed next to me. I nodded my head in response and waited for him to keep talking. "Well, that nigga was making deals, finding out shit, and then letting yo' daddy know when he was finished with them. The police would move in on them niggas, bust them for simple shit like running a red light, or have to do a wellness check on the kids 'cause they wasn't in school. They made the shit look mad random, never letting onto the fact that they were being told all this shit. I remember a couple of times a few people I was going to get into business with got popped for weak ass shit. The hood was buzzing for a while 'cause folks was falling off. I never knew it was the nigga Tika doing it, though."

"This shit is becoming too much," I said, falling back on the bed. I ran my hands over my face and waited to CJ to start back up talking. I just wanted a regular life, one with little to no drama. But that didn't look like it was going to happen.

"Baby, that ain't the worst part of it all," CJ said with a humorless laugh and shake of his head.

"What's the worst part about it all, CJ?" I questioned. I knew whatever he was about to tell me wasn't going to put me in a better mood. If anything, it was about to piss me off.

"That nigga was messing with your friend Red."

"I already knew that part, CJ," I said as I climbed out the

bed. The shit with Tika and my daddy working together wasn't a surprise, either. I'd started putting shit together a few months back. Shit that Tika had said trying to be funny, inside jokes only family would know, he knew about. Spots where my mama or granddaddy used to keep money that only we knew about. Even at his surprise engagement party, when he got in his feelings and started talking. Tika mentioned my daddy way too much to not be working with him.

"How?" he questioned. CJ hopped up out the bed and following me, trying to figure out everything I knew. Basically, waiting for the information to drop so he could pick it up and store it for later. "For real Dove, I thought I was coming in here and telling you shit you ain't know and I find out you already knew and didn't tell me."

"I just been piecing information together, that's all," I said with a shoulder shrug. "It's not like I been holding shit back from you or nothing. Everything I know, I tell you about, so then you know."

"That's 'cause we a team, baby," CJ said as he pulled me to him. Instinctively I wrapped by arms around his waist and rested my face against his chest. "Ain't no secrets going on between us."

I wanted to believe CJ, I really did. But the more I found out with Falcon, the more I realized I didn't know this man or what he was really capable of.

"Dove!" Auntie Constance yelled from the backyard.

I quickly wiped my mouth and splashed water on my face. I could hear everybody in the backyard. My mama being released was one of the best feelings I'd had in a long time. The only thing was, this baby was whooping my ass. I was either nauseous, throwing up, or dead tired. I checked my face in the mirror one last time and left the bathroom. Quickly, I made my way to the kitchen and went looking for my aunt.

"Yes ma'am?" I said once I made it to her outside. Everybody who was important to us was here, friends, family, and a few of my mama's homegirls that she grew up with. And of course, we couldn't leave Chester out if we wanted to. As soon as mama got out, he was at the house waiting. Said if she was out then he was going to make sure she stayed that way. My sisters and I immediately started laughing because the entire car ride to the house we'd told her that Chester would be waiting, and she swore up and down that he wouldn't be. Since her release, my mama hadn't left my house except to go spend time with my sisters or aunts. So, to see her smiling and laughing with her friends made me happy.

"Dove baby, who did CJ have cater this food?" Aunt Constance asked. Immediately I felt the little food I'd eaten earlier start to come back up. Trying my hardest I got myself together and took a deep breath before answering her.

"His cousin Carter owns a BBQ joint on the other side of town. When he told her that we were doing this, she supplied us with the food as a welcome home gesture," I said looking around for Carter. Because she and Benny had gotten into it a few weeks ago over the fact that Benny wasn't sure what he wanted anymore, I wasn't sure if she decided to stay or not.

I knew Benny and Lily were having some problems, but when Carter called her and let her know that Benny was sniffing around her spot, I was pretty sure it was going to be a big ass problem. Surprisingly, Lily took the news well, especially after Carter sent her all the texts and DMs from Benny. Carter had smoothed turned him down and let him know she would be telling his woman everything. Because Benny was a typical man, he thought Carter was bluffing and kept coming at her.

Benny basically told Carter that he felt like dealing with Lily was a mistake and he really wanted her. Lily, again, surprised us all. She didn't cry, scream, or act out. She simply called a sister meeting and let us know she was done with Benny and respected Carter for telling her the truth. That night, she cut Benny off and was living her life to the fullest. It was now Benny running around looking stupid and lost, trying to figure out what was going on with Lily and trying to get her back. None of us were helping him fix it and our men knew nothing about it.

"Oh, that dark-skin girl with the pretty locs?" Constance questioned as she came to stand next to me. "She was here for a little while, but said she had to get back home. Something about her cousin on her mama side people were coming into town and she was excited to see them."

"Yeah, that's Carter," I said with a nod of my head and a small laugh.

Carter had mentioned a few days ago that her cousin Parker and her husband Emanuel would be in town again soon. I'd met them a couple months ago when they'd come into town to check in on Carter and her mother. I was picking up some food for CJ at her restaurant and they were there eating. When I got home, I told CJ and he'd reminded me of a conversation we'd had a few months back about her cousin and her husband being killers. I'd quickly dismissed that notion once I'd met them. Parker was a college professor, and her husband Emanuel owned a few businesses. I'd mention to CJ that Emanuel was looking for a few investors. But he'd quickly turned that idea down, saying that he was trying to stay away from them because of their tempers, and even though the husband came from old money that all money wasn't good money. As if selling drugs and washing it through a couple of his businesses made his dirty money turn into good money. But that wasn't a fight I wanted to have, so I let it go.

"Well, she will be getting more business from us soon 'cause this food is good as hell," Chester said coming up from behind us.

I gave him a sideways church hug and continued looking around the backyard. Lily and Sage stood next to Bleus and Trigga, talking and laughing. Falcon and Mickey weren't too far from them, sitting on the swings, laughing at something in Mickey's phone. CJ stood next to Ms. Clever, more than likely being fussed at about something. My mama and her best friend Tonia sat not too far from us, talking, Tiny sat in the middle of them, eating and watching something on her phone. She'd been out the hospital for a few weeks and was starting to get out the house more. Trigga wasn't letting her out his sight, and only trusted us to be around her. I was happy to see she was enjoying herself despite everything she'd been through.

"I'm sure she'd love that. Tell her I sent you and she will hook you up," I said to Chester as I brought my attention back to him. Out the corner of my eye I watched as Benny made his way through the back door, looking around as if he was searching for someone. It was a shame that they didn't work out, and I wondered if their failed relationship would affect CJ and Benny's friendship. When I mentioned it to CJ, he'd let me know I had nothing to worry about, but I didn't agree with that, either.

Once Benny noticed Lily, he was headed in her direction. But before I could call out to CJ to stop him, shots rang out in the air, making us scatter to make sure we didn't get hit. We knew from past experience that bullets didn't care who or what they hit. Some of us ducked behind what we could, while everybody else dropped to the ground. I was one of the few that hit the ground. Out of instinct, I covered my head with my hands and waited for the shooting to stop. The worst part of it all wasn't the fear of being hit, it was hearing Tiny's screams. She'd been through so much in such a short amount of time, and this was not the type of thing I wanted her to be a part of. Especially after just getting out of the hospital after a year.

"Dove!" CJ yelled as he grabbed me. Instinctively, I wrapped my arms around him. I couldn't cry. I wasn't sure if it was because of the adrenaline running through my veins, or if I'd become numb to the whole gun violence thing, but not one tear dropped from my eyes. "Baby, you okay?"

"Yeah, I'm okay, CJ," I said as I pulled away from him. It wouldn't have mattered if I said anything or not, because he was searching me from head-to-toe. I stepped back a little when he got to my stomach, I still hadn't told him I was pregnant, and this wasn't the time or place to drop that bomb. "Go check on your grandmother."

"You sure?" CJ questioned as he stepped back. His eyes scanned me from head-to-toe again to make sure I wasn't injured. While I loved him for being my protector, I needed him to move his attention to someone else right now. My only reply was a nod of my head. He watched me for a few seconds before turning his attention to Ms. Clever, who was trying to console Tiny who was holding on so tight to her, I'm pretty sure she was cutting off her air supply. This was not how I saw my night going.

The next scream that rang into the air made my blood run cold. Turning around I saw my mama holding Sage against her, rocking back and forth, with tears running down her face. I stumbled as I ran towards her, pushing past overturned chairs and tables. It didn't matter that food was everywhere or that the music somehow could still be heard in the background. All that mattered to me was getting to my sister.

I dropped down next to my mama, who still hadn't let go

of Sage. She gently rubbed her hair out her face and rocked back and forth. My mama's eyes were fixed on Sage's, as if she was trying to sketch it into her memory for later.

"Baby girl, I'm so sorry," Mama said to Sage's lifeless body. "Mama is here, okay? Sage, mama is here."

Someone must've called the police, because shortly afterwards the paramedics came rushing into the backyard, but mama still wouldn't let go of Sage. She pressed her face to Sage's and just cried. I gently palmed my stomach thinking of the baby growing inside of me.

"Mama, you gotta let her go so they can work on her," Falcon said. Gently, Falcon began to remove mama's arms from around Sage. The paramedics quickly took Sage from mama and began checking her out. It was then that I realized how bad it was. Sage had a bullet right in between her eyes and the back of her skull was blown out. She was dead before she even hit the ground.

"Come on baby, you gotta get up," CJ said.

He helped me get up from the ground. Aunt Constance and mama's best friend Faith stood near us, holding onto mama, who was no longer crying. Even though the tears had stopped, mama still looked broken. Bleus held onto Juke for dear life as both of them cried for their own reasons. Juke was afraid and didn't know what was going on while Bleus stood there realizing he'd just lost his best friend and the love of his life.

"Let's get you cleaned up."

It wasn't until CJ spoke again that I looked down at my clothes and realized I was covered in Sage's blood.

Chapter Six

CJ

"I don't care, CJ!" Dove screamed as she moved through the house.

I waited for the explosion that I knew was coming. Just like any other time I left the house and swore I would come back with some type of information, I hadn't. I knew, without a doubt, the fact that I wasn't able to give her some kind of lead towards her sister's killer was starting to affect our relationship. It wasn't anything that Dove said, it was more what she didn't say. Or how she looked at me when I came back home every night. The disappointment was evident each time she looked at me.

It'd been almost a month since the shooting and a little under three weeks since we'd put Sage to rest. I was trying to keep my cool, trying to be the supportive boyfriend in this trying time, but Dove was starting to get on my damn nerves. I get it, she was still mourning, but it wasn't my fault things were going the way they were.

"You swear you're that nigga, CJ, but ain't shit moved! I'm still waiting on answers! You asked my sister to let you handle it! We put our trust in you and you don't have shit!"

"Dove, I'm making moves! You said your damn self that you ain't want to know shit until it was handled," I said as I followed her as she stormed into my office. She looked around before her eyes zoned in on my desk and headed that way. I shook my head in disgust as she pushed folders and papers off my desk. That shit wasn't going to solve anything. If anything, it was going to make it worse. "I'm handling it!"

"How are you handling it?!" She screamed as she turned to face me. I took a step back because I wasn't about to let her get into my face. Woman or not, I didn't play the disrespect shit and she knew that. But, she was getting in my face was pushing buttons I didn't want pressed. The only thing saving her ass right now was that I loved her too much to disrespect her. "I asked you last night if you knew anything, what did you say to me? *I got some shit in the works, mama, don't worry about it.*" Dove took another step forward, closing in the distance I'd put in between us. Her poor attempt of mocking me would've been funny if she wasn't working my damn nerves with all the questions she had. "Don't worry about it? Nigga that was my fucking sister! I'm supposed to worry! Just like if that was Benny in the ground, you'd be worried. Hell, you'd be tearing up the fucking city trying to figure this shit out."

"I do have shit in place!" I yelled back to her. Fuck it, if she wanted that street nigga that everybody knew about, then she could have him. "I been in the streets! I been asking questions and putting feelers out to see if somebody been talking and guess what? They ain't saying shit! Whoever came after us that day came after us on some solo shit! They didn't go running they fucking mouth. They shot up our backyard, ditched the stolen car in the woods, and torched that shit! They covering their tracks completely."

"That don't make sense, CJ! This shit just doesn't feel right at all! The streets are always talking, always moving for something or someone with money. Information can be bought. Put a bullet in somebody head for all I care, but I want that shit with my sister handled or I'm going to let someone else handle that shit!"

"Who you got to handle something, Dove, huh?" I said with a smirk on my face. "Ain't no damn body gonna step up and handle shit that was basically handled by a damn ghost!"

I let out a humorless laugh as I watched her take a step back and roll her eyes. She knew I was telling the truth. Not a damn soul was going to talk if they didn't know what was going on. Yeah, a few folks would make some shit up to get any kind of money I put out there, but that shit wasn't going to lead to anything. I'd already put a bullet in a few niggas' heads 'cause they lied about the information that they gave. Now people knew not to play. If their information wasn't 100% accurate, then they didn't say anything. "You so fucking mad at me for something I didn't do! Some shit that more than likely ain't got shit to do with me!"

"What?" Dove questioned. Her eyebrows damn near shot to the top of her forehead in surprise before her face went completely blank. "You think this got something to do with us? What the fuck we do, CJ? The streets been talking and you ain't said shit?"

"Yo mama just got out of jail, Dove. Folks been talking since everything went down. Between yo' mama and daddy, and let's not mention yo' sister, baby, folks been talking! You and your people ain't innocent! Folks looking for your pops. Falcon and Mickey drop bodies without a second thought. Bleus right behind they ass. I swear every time I turn around, Trigga calling me 'cause he need another spot cleaned up. Hell, the cleaners are doubling they price right now 'cause of how yo' people moving. You really trying to tell me you think folks ain't talking?! The streets watching any and everybody that last name is Lincoln or is associated with y'all."

"Including you, huh?" Dove said with a laugh as she nodded her head. "The streets been checking for the Lincolns 'cause they don't understand how we moved. They don't know our loyalty ain't shit to play with, right? My mama just was doing a bid that ain't have shit to do with her. She held it down when a nigga was running his mouth doing bitch shit. We ain't innocent, we don't pretend to be. But Sage ain't do shit to nobody. She took care of her child and lived her life. What if that shit was me, CJ? What if I was just taking care of our child and living life and somebody put a bullet in between my eyes like they did my sister? Would you be okay with it or would you ride hard for me like Bleus riding for her? Could you look at our baby and know that you tried your hardest and so did my people? Or would you just keep living? 'Cause right now I don't see a fucking problem with what Bleus, Falcon, and Mickey doing."

"Man look, you trippin'. I get that you're mourning the loss of your sister, but you're adding variables to this shit that ain't got shit to do with us," I said with a shake of my head as I started to pick up the paper she'd knocked over. "I'm working as hard as I can to find out who did this shit. I said when I find out who did it, I would tell you. If you can't let me do that shit in peace, then you a fucking problem I don't need!"

"I'm a problem you don't need?" Dove questioned. "Now, I'm a problem?"

"Yeah, you a fucking problem, Dove. I can't move too damn hard and make too much damn noise 'cause I already got the cops on my back. Did you forget I was pulled into the station not too long ago? They were asking questions about your ass! Not me! The shit hot around you and yo' people, not mine!" I dropped the papers onto the desk and turned to face her. The little tears she had running down her face didn't do shit for me and I let her know just that. "Keep them tears to yourself. You want to talk big bad shit one minute then play the victim the next. Keep that same energy when I give it back to you."

"You really fuckin funny, CJ," Dove said with a shake of her head. "You can't move in the streets like you want to and you can't admit that shit. I became the problem, but nah baby, I ain't it. Yeah, shit hot around my people right now, but you was being pulled into that station long before this went down. Silas stay picking your ass up from there 'cause you got cocky as hell. You thought because you was dealing with a Lincoln you could move like you was one, and that shit ain't as easy as you thought. You can't figure the shit out 'cause this shit is above your reach. TCB can't handle this shit. But don't worry, I know somebody who can."

"Damn I said I would figure this shit out! Either let me do that shit or let your ghost of a person do that shit!"

"Say less," Dove said as she turned and walked out the room. A part of me wanted to go after her, but I knew to let her cool down first. She was hurting, I'd let the disrespect fall to the wayside this time.

I dropped in my chair with a deep sigh and tried to figure out what was going on. I had to be missing something. There was no way that the streets weren't talking. I knew better than anyone how this shit worked, Dove and her family were too big to not be making noise. This shit should've been the only thing going around, but like I told Dove, it wasn't. Nobody was saying a damn word. The sound of the garage door opening pulled me out my thoughts. Pulling it up on my computer, I watched as Dove's car pulled out the driveway.

Pressing the rewind button, I watched as Dove angrily threw a bag into her trunk and slammed it shut. She picked up her carrier container off the hood of her car as she passed it, then damn near pulled the passenger door off the hinge.

From the way she was moving, I could tell she was on the phone. I watched as she gently sat the carrier into the car and then slammed her door shut. No matter how mad she was at the situation, she wasn't about to abuse her damn pet. I finally pressed the button to allow me to hear into garage.

"No, he said I was the fucking problem. Matter fact, he said we were the problem. Why the fuck would I be here if he can't understand what I am going through. I just put my sister in the ground!" Dove said as she yanked her driver door open. "That shit is selfish! Sage body ain't even cold yet and he worried about the damn police pulling him into the station. Hell, for the last year he's been pulled in more times than I can count. Each and every time he's walked his ass out with a smirk on his face and an extra swag in his step. But we're the fucking problem." Dove paced back and forth next to her car. Whoever she was talking to was trying to talk some sense into her. Dove was trippin'. Yeah, I said they were the problem, but she had to know that shit wasn't meant in the negative. I just moved different from how they did. At times, her sister was almost careless, that's why Mickey had to clean up behind her so much. It was like she didn't give a damn, or maybe at times, she wanted to get caught.

"Nah, fuck him, mommy," Dove said. "He can worry about his self for a while. I gotta worry about myself and not stressing myself out. I have this baby to worry about, and if its daddy thinks we a problem now, who the hell knows what he will think once he or she is here?" She stood there for a few seconds nodding her head before she hung up the phone. Dove dropped her head down and rubbed her stomach, without looking back she got into her car and drove off.

Jumping up from my seat, I ran into our bedroom looking for my keys to go after her. I damn near dropped to the ground when I realized all her shit was gone. She'd packed up everything, all of her drawers were empty, and her side of the closet was bare. I grabbed a pair of Jordans out the closet, my keys, and raced down the garage. Wasn't no way in hell Dove was leaving me. Especially if she was carrying my baby.

Chapter Seven

DOVE

"Dove!" CJ yelled as he pulled into the driveway behind my truck. "Where the hell you thinking you going?"

I didn't even look back at him as I pulled my key from my pocket. If he wanted to cause a scene, he'd be the only one acting in it. I was too tired to deal with his shit or his attitude, especially after he just pretty much told me we were the reason for my sister's death. "I know you hear me talking to you."

"I hear you talking CJ, I just don't want to deal with it right now. I'm tired, my feet hurt, and I'm starting to get a headache," I replied. Out the corner of my eye I watched him jump out his car without even turning it off. I turned around and gave him my complete attention as he stormed up the walkway towards me. Even with him going off, I wasn't afraid of him. If anything, the pissed off look turned me on. "I'm about to go in the house, CJ. Call me when you ready to talk to me civilized."

"Oh my goodness, Dove. Do you hear yourself?! You'll talk to me when I'm ready to act civilized?! You so fucking foul, man!" CJ said as he threw his hands in the air in frustration. "You ain't even gonna deny you pregnant, are you? How long have you known, huh? Shit, was you even going to tell me?!"

"CJ," I said with a deep sigh as I shook my head.

"Was you even gonna keep my baby or was you gonna abort it?" CJ said interrupting me before I could say anything else besides his name.

"What?!" I said as I dropped my bag in the chair next to the door. "What kind of woman do you think I am? Of course, I was going to tell you, but then shit got out of hand! My brother popping back up, my mama getting out of jail, Sage being killed, you going back and forth to the damn police station. For the last six weeks, I haven't had a moment of peace! How the fuck can I celebrate a life coming into this world when I'm mourning my sister being taken out of it?"

I watched CJ for a moment before shaking my head. He didn't get it. He was so used to dealing with death and moving on with his life that he didn't get that I'm not sure how to move on with my life. I was used to a simple life. Even though my family ran the streets, I didn't, and this was too much for me.

"I just need a moment, give me that. It's all I'm asking."

"You got a few days, Dove. That's all I'm giving you to give yourself some time to figure this out, and then I'm coming back to get you. I don't care if I have to drag you back kicking and screaming, you and my child will be under the same roof that I am," CJ said before he turned and walked back to his car. He didn't give me a second glance before he pulled off. His music bumped hard against his speakers as he made his way down the street.

Shaking my head, I turned back to see my mama standing in the doorway with a big ass goofy smile on her face. My mama pulled me into a hug I didn't know I needed and I rested my head on her shoulder.

"What did I tell you the first time you told me about him?" Mama questioned as she rubbed my back. I thought back to our conversation while she was still in jail. When she'd call me for her weekly check in, I couldn't stop running my mouth about him. Everything he did and stood for was everything I wanted in a man.

"You said he would either be my greatest downfall or my biggest blessing," I replied as I raised my head up to look her in the eyes. "You said I loved too hard and even though I wasn't ready to admit it to myself, I was in love with him after spending one night with him."

"Then what did I tell you when I met him in person," she questioned as she held my face in between her hands. Using her thumb, she wiped tears I didn't even realize had fallen from my eyes.

"That he was everything you ever envisioned in a partner for me. I just have to know how to love him the way he needs to be loved, because he already knows how to love me."

"Right, now listen to me and listen well, because I'm only going to say this one time," Mama said. She waited for me to nod my head before she kept talking. "That man is not one to play with. He is a man and will only allow so much disrespect before he walks away. I can tell by just looking at him. And Dove, you hurt him. Grieve for you sister baby, but don't grieve so hard that you lose yourself. He had every right to know about that child that is growing inside of you the minute you found out. Apologize to him, and when push comes to shove and he finds out who killed your sister, stand next to him when he put a bullet in their head. 'Cause baby, ain't no doubt in my mind that he is going to make it his mission to find out."

Chapter Eight

RED

"Bitch, you think I give a fuck about her sister being dead?" I asked my cousin Cora as I rolled my blunt. I had to play off the fact like I didn't know what was going on with Dove. The hood didn't know who'd shot at her and her people and put her sister in the ground. For the last year, I'd been making moves in the shadows, any and everything I'd been working was finally starting to fall into place. A bitch was happy as hell, but I couldn't show it too much. "That bitch played me for that nigga CJ and I ain't like her sister no damn way."

"She played you?" Cora asked with a laugh. She pushed her long, wavy weave out her face and rolled her eyes at me as she put on her makeup. I wanted to ask her ass why she was trying so hard to cover up her raggedy ass skin, but I was going to keep my mouth shut. "Was you not the bitch that set her up with the nigga you stayed fucking?"

"Girl, you talking about something you don't know about," I said. I wanted to deny that shit so bad, but Cora knew better than anyone how the shit with Tika and Dove went down. She was the one who gave me the idea of hooking her up with someone so I could keep tabs. When I mentioned Tika, she'd told me no and that it would blow up in my face. She was right, but I wasn't going to admit that shit, either.

"You wish I didn't," Cora said with a laugh. "Yo' ass right in yo' raggedy ass feelings 'cause that nigga ended up falling in love with her and you sitting over there with his baby and nothing else. Shit, didn't that nigga get another chick pregnant, too?" With a laugh Cora got up from her seat and went to her closet. She went through her closet without looking back at me. "You need to call that girl or at least text her and tell her you got them in your prayers or something. I know my granddaddy went to the service 'cause he nosy as shit and said it was nice as hell. They mama was there, too, looking like the black ghetto royalty she is."

"Fuck her mama, too," I said with a roll of my eyes. I couldn't stand Rose Lincoln. Hell, I think I hated her more than I did her daughters. From the time I could remember, everybody talked about how dope Rose was, how she was one of the realest bitches out there. Then she started fucking with Mister and then everybody thought they were Gods. "That bitch should've got a bullet, too."

"Girl you trippin' hard as hell now," Cora said looking over shoulder at me. "You wish death on that girl whole damn family? For the fuck what? 'Cause Dove and them ain't ever did shit to you."

"Why you all of sudden #TeamLincoln? Wasn't you fucking with Mister? If anything, you should be saying fuck them too, 'cause that nigga would do you dirty if Rose called him," I said as I got up to check on my baby, who was sleep in his car seat next to the bed.

When all the shit with Tika went down, I dipped out in the middle of the night. I didn't know I was pregnant, but I knew that if they found Tika, it wouldn't take them long to find me. So, I went to visit some family on my daddy's side in New Mexico. I spent my entire pregnancy in the house, and when I had the baby, I didn't tell anybody except my mama. She begged me to come home but understood why I'd stayed gone. Once the heat had died down, I snuck my ass right back into town in the dead of night. Over the past few months, I only visited a few people, Cora being one of them. He looked so much like Tika it was often times scary. I know if Tika was still here, that Titus would be his pride and joy. All he ever talked about was having a son. Don't get me wrong, he loved his daughter, but it was something about him wanting to have a son that drove him. Each time we had sex, he would say he hoped that he got me pregnant, and I gave him a son.

"That nigga loves Rose, ain't no denying that shit. Even now, if someone asks him if he loves that woman, he will tell you 'yeah' without a second thought. I ain't got no beef with her. She didn't know about me and just did what a main bitch was supposed to do. She checked up on her nigga and he would come running. I can't be mad at that shit," Cora said as she pulled a denim off-the-shoulder jumpsuit from the closet and put it on. "Plus, that nigga was wrong for messing with my young ass back in the day. He knew I was in the same grade as Falcon. Nigga was pulling a straight R. Kelly."

"And your nasty ass loved it," I said with an eye roll.

Her only response was to laugh as she walked out the room. I pulled my phone out the side pocket of the diaper bag and checked my social media. A couple of my cousins had sent me a message, but I wasn't interested in dealing with them right now. I threw the phone in my purse, picked up Titus's car seat and diaper bag, and took him to Cora's mama's room. She'd agreed to watch him until my mama got off work so Cora and I could go hang out for a while. I was ready to make my presence known in the city and the best place to do that was at a Focus concert.

———

I could feel the vibration of the music though the floor as we moved through the crowd. Focus had just got off stage, and like always, he'd killed it. Now the club was clearing out, but they had his music on repeat to keep the crowd from tearing up the place. I'd seen so many people and chopped it up like old times, the only thing that pissed me off was everyone asking me about Dove. Sis was not my concern, and the quicker they got that through their heads, the better.

"Red, baby girl, where you been?" Said a voice behind me. I didn't even turn around. It didn't matter who it was and if I hadn't talked to them in over a year, there wasn't a point to stop and talk to them now.

"Cora, I'm hungry as hell," I said as I pulled my keys out my pocket to unlock the door. From the looks of things everyone was headed to the local BBQ joint that was down the street. "If you're down for it, I can go for some wings."

"May as well, I need to put some food on my stomach," Cora said as she put her seat belt on.

The drive down to the BBQ joint was short. When we got there, we quickly changed out of our heels and threw a pair of tennis shoes on. The time for being cute was over, we were now getting comfortable so we could drink and eat some good food. Once we were changed, we got out the car and headed inside to order our food. Because it was the summer, and the weather was nice, we didn't have a problem sitting outside. Plus, it gave us a chance to check out our surroundings. Niggas liked to get trigger happy in the summer, so if we needed to move quickly there were no walls keeping us in place.

"Oh, look, it's that nigga Benny," Cora said.

She nodded her head in the direction of the restaurant entrance. I turned in my seat and watched as a tall, dark-skinned dude came through the door. He was talking to another nigga I'd never seen before, but my eyes stayed on Benny. He was a good-looking dude. Even though I didn't usually mess with bigger dudes, I could tell he had some money and I always messed with niggas that had money.

"He cute, look like he got a little money," I said turning my attention back to Cora.

"Bitch, you like playing with fire, don't you?" Cora questioned with a laugh.

"What you mean?" I questioned as I turned back to look at Benny.

"Benny is second or third in command of the TCB. That nigga is CJ's right-hand man," Cora said with another laugh. I sized Benny up again. He looked like a nigga that hustled, from his designer jeans to his jewelry. Him being CJ's right-hand man didn't scare me. I didn't want a relationship with him, just information. I planned to fuck up Dove and CJ's life a little bit more, and they'd never expect the information to come from someone CJ trusted. "Plus, if I remember right, he used to mess with Dove's sister Lily."

"They broke up?" I questioned. I turned back to face Cora, so it didn't look like I was staring at him. Honestly, I didn't care if they were together or not, I was still going to fuck him.

"Yeah," Cora said with a shrug of her shoulders. "Word on the street is he was trying to fuck with the owner of this place. Her name Carter, I think, but I'm not 100% sure about that. Lily found out and kicked his ass to the curb. Big ass nigga just be around here sulking now 'cause Carter don't want his ass and he ain't got nowhere to go."

"Well, excuse me real quick," I said. I didn't give Cora a

chance to respond before I got up out my seat and made my way to Benny. He was sitting at a table with a few people, but he didn't look too interested in the conversation 'cause his head was in his phone.

"Big boy, you too fine to be sitting here looking so sad," I said sitting down next to him. Benny looked up from his phone and smiled at me. He didn't give me the pathetic vibe, just more so he knew he fucked up, and didn't know how to fix it. But that was a good thing for me, he could be heartbroken all he wanted. I wasn't worried about his ass, and more than likely once I was done with his ass, CJ would put a damn bullet in his head.

"Nah baby, I ain't sad," Benny said with a shake of his head as he put his phone away.

I smirked as I watched him check me out. Even in a pair of Jordan's and an all-black romper, I looked better than majority of the women out here. My signature blue hair was replaced with some waist length box braids that I had pulled in a bun. My makeup looked natural, and my nails were short because of the baby. My shape had almost filled out. Before Titus I was a size six, now I rocked my extra weight from the baby with pride. I was now a size ten. I'd lost my stomach, but my thighs and titties looked good as hell.

"Then, what got you over here chillin' with a group of niggas when you could have walked up to my table and sat down with me," I questioned with a smile. I batted my eyes a little and bit into my bottom lip. "I mean, I noticed you when you walked out here, so I know you noticed me too."

"Yeah baby, I saw you, but I wasn't trying to interrupt your dinner with your homegirl," Benny said nodding his head in the direction of Cora, who was now talking to some random older nigga. "But it looks like her attention elsewhere now."

"Yeah, it does. So, what's going on with you?" I questioned

as I stood. "You trying to get out of here and get to know each other better?"

"You ain't said nothing but a word, baby," Benny said as he stood. Up close he was a lot taller than I thought he was. I stood near five-nine, and he had almost a foot over me in height. "You and your homegirl ride together?"

"Yeah, she rode with me," I said as I adjusted my top. Benny didn't even act like he wasn't looking at my titties. He smiled when his eyes met mine.

"Drop your keys with her, I'll make sure you get home," Benny said. "Meet me in the front, I gotta close out my tab, then we can get out of here." I nodded my head and then headed back to Cora.

"Alright, don't fuck my car up," I said dropped my keys down on the table. Cora didn't even act like she didn't know the deal, she grabbed my keys and put them in her purse. I grabbed my own bag and phone as I prepared to leave.

"I hope you know what you doing fucking with that nigga. Benny ain't one to take being played lightly. That nigga will kill you," Cora said with the shake of her head.

"I got this shit. Just enjoy yourself and get home safely. My mama already texted me and told me she got Titus so I'm good until tomorrow afternoon."

"Alright now, remember what I said," Cora said. I gave her a quick hug and headed towards the front.

Benny was sitting in his all-black Range Rover with all the windows down. Just like earlier, his attention was on his phone as music Focus music blasted through the speaker. I knew better than to just open his door, so I tapped on the door to get his attention. He looked up from his phone, then unlocked the door. I climbed into the car and shut the door. Benny reached over and turned the music down.

"Say little mama, what did you say your name was again?" Benny questioned as he pulled out the parking lot.

"I didn't" I said reaching over to unzip his pants. He watched me with a smirk on his face as he let me pull his dick out his pants. "Don't crash," I said before putting his dick in my mouth. I felt the car jerk slightly as I went to work. This nigga better not kill us before I get the information I needed.

Chapter Nine

DOVE

"Mama, you not even listening," I said. I'd been at our old house for nearly three days, and each day when I made it to the living room, my mama would ask me when I was going home. And each time I would tell her I was home, and she'd remind me my home was with CJ.

"Dove, what do you mean I'm not listening?" Mama questioned as she put the final touches on the French toast she was making.

Since she'd been out of jail, she'd cooked each of her meals. The only time she allowed us to order anything was for her get-together. Mama sprinkled some powder and brown sugar mix over her food, then looked up at me with a raised eyebrow. Even though she'd been gone for a few years, she hadn't lost her touch in the kitchen. Each meal was, in my opinion, over the top each time she cooked. But I wasn't going to tell her that because I enjoyed each one. The fact that they were nothing short of a five-course meal for each sitting was only a plus.

"I've told already, I'm home," I said as I sat at the island. I was no longer nauseous and had hit the constant hunger phase of pregnancy. So, any time she was the kitchen, I was right there waiting.

"Dove, listen to me and listen good, this ain't your home. Your home is with that man, and don't get me wrong, as much as I love having you here and watching you feed my grandchild every chance you get, I am tired of looking at your face. I want to walk around this house naked and if I want to have company, I want to be able to moan and scream his name without the fear of my child hearing us," Mama said. I stared at her for a second and then dropped my head into my hands. Growing up, my mama never minced her words for us, we always knew where we stood with her and if we weren't sure, she would definitely let us know. So, I wasn't surprised at what she'd just said, I was more shocked that it had taken her three days to admit it.

"Mama, ain't nobody trying to hear you yell out Chester's name," Falcon said coming into the kitchen with Juke right behind her. Since Sage's death, we'd been splitting custody over him, and it was my turn to keep him for a few days. When he wasn't with us, he was with Bleus. Legally he was named as Juke's father since it was his name on the birth certificate. But he knew we needed time with him, so Bleus agreed to our request.

"Who the hell said it was Chester's name I'd be yelling out?" Mama questioned as she picked Juke up. I smiled as I watched him study Mama's face. Out of all of us, Sage looked the most like her. So, I knew that each time he looked at Mama, he was looking at his mama.

"Girl, who else name you gonna be screaming out?" Falcon questioned with a laugh. "Ain't no other nigga coming over here every day but him."

"Right, don't play with Chester like that. You know he think he's your boo," I said with a laugh as she twisted her face up at Falcon and me. "That man looked out for us the entire time you were away. I don't know how many times he'd just pop up and be ready to go off if he didn't like how something looked or he swore the vibe was off."

"Nigga was being a daddy to us for as long as I can remember. Even before you were locked up," Falcon said with shrug. "Shit, for a while I had to remind him that he wasn't our daddy, 'cause he was going off on any and everybody that stepped to us."

"Nah, that nigga Mister is the only one that ever went raw with me," Mama said. "If I was smart, I would've let Chester do it. But I thought I was in love with Mister, and you know how women act when they are in love with a nigga."

"They can treat us like shit, and we will still wash they dirty draws," I said with a shake of my head. "I don't know how many times Tika did me dirty and I let him come back without a second thought."

"'Cause you was young, dumb, and in love," Mama said her own shake of her head. "Now you got a good man begging to talk to you and you won't give him the time of day."

"'Cause he said we were the problem," I said with a huff. "Basically, he said we were the reason for Sage's death."

"That ain't what he said Dove, don't lie on that man like that," Mama said as she made Juke's plate. "He said we were the problem, but he didn't blame none of the stuff with Sage on us. He was frustrated and so were you. Some shit was said but y'all didn't mean it. Now you're being stubborn and don't want to talk to him 'cause you know you were just as wrong as he was."

"Mama, you supposed to be TeamDove, not TeamCJ," I said, not denying anything she said.

The fact that my mama and CJ got along from the moment they met didn't go unnoticed. The only two men she ever took to like that were Bleus and Mickey, and she even gave them a hard time when we were younger 'cause she knew that they were sniffing behind Falcon and Sage. She always said she wanted us to be with someone she could respect and that treated us right. She said from the moment she put her hand in CJ's, she knew he was the man for me.

"Baby, I will always be TeamDove 'cause you and your sisters popped out my hot box." I turned to Falcon who stood next to the stove with the same lost look on her face as I'm sure I had. This woman just said whatever she thought. "But your stubborn ass needs to realize you were just as wrong as he was. He can admit his faults, but you can't. How you gonna show your child what a grown woman does when you can't even admit you in the wrong? That baby gonna be stubborn just like you but look just like him 'cause you always mad at him."

"And you gonna be babysitting so you gonna suffer," I said with shrug of my shoulders.

"Which is fine with me, as long as you living back in that house with him," Mama said. She picked up Juke's plate from the counter and walked out the kitchen, leaving Falcon and me.

"You know she right, though, don't you?" Falcon said as she began to make her own plate. "Eventually, you're going to have to tuck your tail in between your legs and head on home. He already went off on you for not telling him that you were pregnant. Mama called me cracking up, talking about you met your match with him 'cause he ain't give a damn about shit about how mad you thought you were. He gave you a few days to calm down, but you coming home and him taking care of y'all baby."

"Yeah, I can't front, that shit turned me on a little," I said with a laugh as I got up from my seat. "Had me ready to drop down on my knees and suck his dick right then and there."

Falcon and I sat in silence as we ate our food. There were things about my sister that I didn't get. She was hard with most people, didn't let them get to know her, and stayed to herself. Growing up I thought it was because she didn't like too many people, but I later found out that wasn't the truth. She was really just trying to protect us. She became the killer, so we didn't have to be.

God knows how much I love my mama, but she raised us all different, and even though we were basically stairstep babies, we all got different sides to her. Falcon got the tough side. She was Mama's rider. For as far back as I could remember, she was in the passenger side of mama's car going on runs with her. She learned the business, so we didn't have to get mixed up in it. I got a softer version, she taught me to cook, played games with me, and pushed my curiosity of animals to the forefront. I went to every after-school program, camp, and summer course I could. Sage's version was different from mine. Mama taught her how to be a woman. They went and got their nails and hair done on a regular basis. Mama dressed Sage like the Barbie doll she was. She taught her about her femininity and how it was a gift from above. Then there was Lily, who was pushed to be everything we didn't want to be. She got to explore the world, travel because the wind blew her a certain direction. I often times thought that Lily was a hippie, from the way she dressed to the way she lived. There was no limit to her appeal on people, so everyone wanted to be around her.

Mama loved us differently, but treated us the same. She gave us what we needed in life in order to survive. Her only mistake was loving a man who didn't love her back. Mister loved the opportunity my mama gave him. His actions showed that and I'm not even talking about the jail thing. I'm more so focused on the cheating that he did. Mister had two other kids by two different women and countless women he made have abortions while he was with my mama. Those two kids were a constant reminder that our mama deserved better but didn't realize it.

"Can I ask you a question?" I said to Falcon as I finished off my food. She nodded her head, but didn't look up from her plate. "What made you fall for Mickey?"

"Mickey made me fall for Mickey," Falcon replied with a smile as she looked up at me. Falcon came off as cold to so many, but when she talked about Mickey, it was like a switch was flipped and her entire demeanor changed. "Mickey saw me before I did, if that makes any sense. From the first day of eighth grade when I got kicked out of class for fighting those twins, he was right by my side. They didn't expect his nerdy-looking ass to be able to get down like that."

"And you did?" I questioned with a laugh as I washed my plate.

"Hell no! Do you remember what Mickey looked like back then? He was maybe seventy pounds soaking wet, had those pop bottle glasses, and braces. And when he pulled his shirt off and his little wife beater was hanging off his body, I even laughed. But then he started swinging and I quickly realized his ass wasn't a punk. My baby was throwing them haymakers and not asking no questions," Falcon said with a laugh as she pushed her plate towards me to wash.

I laughed along with her because I remembered that day vividly. Mama came up to the school with a whole attitude, ready to go off on Falcon because just that morning she had told her not to be fighting. When I saw her storming down the hallway towards the office, I followed right behind her. Mainly, because I was nosy and wanted to see her go off on Falcon, and because I'd heard all about the fight during lunch. Everybody wanted to know why Falcon and the nerdy new boy had beat up the twins. I didn't have an answer because I didn't know. It turned out she fought them because over the summer they'd told some of their friends that they'd seen Falcon naked. When she found out about it, she'd told our mama who'd went down to their mama and cursed her out. But that wasn't enough for Falcon, so she'd decided on her way to school that she was going to fight them.

"But you knew Mickey was the one, though, right?" I questioned as I turned off the water. I turned around and gave Falcon my full attention because I wanted to know the answer. "Like, was there every anyone else?"

"It feels like I've always loved Mickey. He completes me. There has never been someone I loved more than him," Falcon said with a shake of her head. "But I have loved other people. It's just different with him. Mickey completes me, calms me, makes me want to do better."

"And the other guy?" I questioned as I thought back to the people Falcon had dated in the past.

"Mateo fueled my anger. He pushed me to be more deadly when I just wanted to be loved. Mommy taught me how to be dangerous, I didn't need that from a man."

"Mateo was controlling. As long as you were showing out and killing people, he was happy," I said to her. Falcon nodded but didn't say anything. "Mickey made you a better person. He pushed you to be more than what the world saw you as."

"Right," Falcon said as she got up from her seat. Like always, she was dressed in a pair of black sweats that she paired with a fitted grey t-shirt and black and grey Nike's. "But here's the secret with Mickey. He never feared me or what I can do. If anything, I think it's a turn-on for him. He knows how dangerous I am, yet he knows he's more dangerous. They just don't realize it because of how he carries himself. We balance each other's crazy."

Chapter Ten

CJ

I cocked my gun but didn't say anything as I made my way through the strip club. I'd been helping my Benny's Uncle with some paperwork in his office when they front door called up and said I had a visitor. No one knew I was here, and I knew that Dove was at her Mama's still licking her wounds. So, no one should have been looking for me. I nodded at Tatum as I passed her. Since it was early in the day, I knew she was only here to teach someone a routine.

"Aye Manny, who looking for me?" I asked the security as I tucked my gun into my pants. I looked around the room and didn't seen anyone.

"Nigga outside, CJ," Manny said as he pointed to the door. "You know if I don't know them, I don't let folks in here if it ain't regular business hours."

"He leave a name?" I questioned as I slapped Manny up and pulled him into a quick hug. Manny was a real one. He'd been working at the club for almost four years. Unc had given him a job straight out of prison, saying that he'd helped him out a few times on the yard, so he was repaying a favor.

"Yeah, said his name is Memphis. He should be over by

the trees near a black Charger," Manny said as he moved past me to head towards the back to do his normal security sweep. I nodded at Manny and then headed out the door. I looked around, and just like Manny said, there was a man standing next to an all-black 2021 Hellcat Challenger.

"You looking for me?" I questioned as I made my way towards Memphis. The closer I got the more I realized how much he looked like Falcon and Dove. This was their older brother, the one that Dove feared and Falcon hated. Immediately, I had my guard up with him.

"Yeah man, I been looking for you," Memphis said as he blew smoke from his mouth and crossed his arms. "I wanted to know if you knew who killed my sister?"

I let out a small laugh and shook my head. This nigga was really here questioning me about his sister's death, but from what I heard he didn't even deal with them like that. When I asked Dove about him and their other sibling, she said that Memphis was like a ghost in the wind. They didn't know where he lived or what he did for a living, but every so often he would pop his head up and make a little noise, then be gone just as fast.

"Nigga, are you really here asking me that shit?" I questioned. I didn't even give him enough respect to look at him. I watched as a black Honda drove by. I nodded at the driver, who looked vaguely familiar, but didn't think too much about it.

"That was my sister, hell yeah I'm asking," Memphis said. "Look, I know my sisters don't think too much of me, but I always had they back and wanted the best for them. If you ain't got shit on who did this, then just say that so I can start making some noise. Folks start talking when I start moving."

"Nigga, you ain't got no fucking pull," I said with a laugh as I pulled my blunt from behind my ear. "I been out here for the last month working to find out what the fuck going on and you think just 'cause you popped your head out the sand that people will starting moving?" I took a pull of my blunt and released the smoke through my nose. "Hell, you know what, if you think you can do better than me, then please go ahead and do it."

"Say less," Memphis said as he pulled his keys from his pocket.

"Aye, Memphis, just understand that shit don't happen in this city without me knowing about it," I said to him. Memphis nodded his head as he pulled open his car door and got in.

"You know what I hate about niggas like you, CJ??" Memphis said with a laugh of his own after he rolled down his car window. "You think people just supposed to respect you because you said so. Nigga, I already know you ain't did shit to get the rank you got. That big nigga Benny you hang with do all the fucking work and you just the face of this shit." Memphis pulled another blunt out and lit it.

"Nigga, you don't know shit about what the fuck I do."

"You keep thinking that shit, my nigga. But just some words of advice. Be careful who you telling all yo' business to. These niggas pillow talk more than these bitches do. When you ready to put in some work, let me know. 'Cause if you think Falcon deadly with that thang you ain't seen shit yet."

Without letting me get another word in, Memphis rolled his window up and rolled off. I watched his car pull out the parking lot and go down the street before I pulled my phone out and dialed a number.

"Aye Benny, where you at my nigga?" I pulled my shorts up some and headed to my own car. "Bet, lets link up."

Chapter Eleven

BENNY

"Give me like twenty minutes," I said into the phone as I watched shorty from last night walk out the bathroom. She smiled at me but didn't say anything when she realized I had my phone to my ear. "Man, you know what, give me a hour. I gotta take care of this shit that just popped up."

I hung up the phone and grabbed my hard dick. All shorty did was walk out the bathroom and I was ready for another round. From the minute she hopped into the car and started sucking my dick as I drove, I knew she wasn't going to be on the bullshit. We went round-for-round last night and early this morning. Anything I wanted to try, she was down for it. At one point, I had her ass hoisted up on the hood of my truck and was fucking her outside.

"You gotta go?" Re'Gine asked. It took a few times, but I finally got her to agree to tell me what to call her. Her constantly hesitating let me know it was her real name, but I didn't give a damn as long as she kept sucking my dick and letting me fuck her like she was.

"Nah, not yet," I said as I pulled my dick out my shorts. Re'Gine's eyes dropped down to my dick and she licked her lips. "I told my homebody I had to handle something real quick before I met up with him." Re'Gine dropped her towel and climbed into my lap. I could already feel how wet her fat ass pussy was when she sat down on me.

"I thought we had a few more hours," Re'Gine said as she stroked my shit.

When she rubbed the tip against her clit, I groaned in pleasure. As much as I loved being in control, I loved it more when a woman took what she wanted, and Re'Gine had no problem doing just that. I leaned forward and pulled one of her hard nipples into my mouth, rolling it between my lips before letting it go. Last night when I did that, and milk flew out that bitch, I almost went off. Then she explained she had a baby at home and was still pumping for him, so I let that shit slide. But after that, I started hitting it raw. Bitches can't get pregnant while breast feeding. And I couldn't get enough of feeling how Re'Gine's pussy responded to my dick without the condom.

"We got time for another round or two, but then I gotta handle some business," I said as Re'Gine slid down on my dick. I gripped her ass with both hands and helped her find the perfect rhythm. "Shit, I may need a little longer than that. For the next two hours, I fucked Re'Gine like I'd never touch another piece of pussy again.

"Benny, nigga you said a hour, shit it's been almost three," CJ said as he looked up from his laptop. I shrugged my shoulders but didn't say anything about it. Once Re'Gine and I got into a rhythm, it was hard to break it. Her pussy felt too good to be running away from it and come talk shop. Especially since I knew the conversation was going to be centered around Dove and her sisters. Since Lily broke up with me and her sister's death, I hadn't had anything to do with the Lincoln sisters. Don't get me wrong, I felt bad for them having to bury Sage, but that shit wasn't my problem anymore.

"Shit, I been busy with this new shorty name Re'Gine and loss track of time," I said with a shrug as I sat down. I crossed my arms over my chest and waited for his reply. Instead of a smart-ass comment, CJ just sat closed his laptop and nodded his head.

"Well, you and Re'Gine gonna need to chill out for a minute so we can figure this shit out," CJ said with a little attitude.

"Nigga, you and Dove still must be at it 'cause you trippin' too hard for no reason. I chill with shorty for one night and then all of a sudden it's a problem," I said with a nod of my head as I thought back on the last month. Anytime he and Dove got into it, this nigga would be trippin' with everybody. It wasn't until they got back on right terms that he would come back and apologize. "But what's the deal? You need something?"

"Don't worry about what me and my girl got going on," CJ said dismissively. Because of the fact he didn't deny what I said, I knew I'd hit the nail on the head. "Yeah, I wanted to know if you'd heard anything about the shooting?" CJ questioned. He rested back in his chair and just watched me. CJ was the type of nigga that was hard to read at times, you never knew how he was feeling until he wanted you to. "I told Dove I was working on it, but with the police on my back I'm trying to stay low."

"Not too much of anything," I said with a shrug of my shoulders as I pulled my phone out my pants pocket. "I talked with Bleus and Trigga the other night and they said the same thing we been saying. Whoever did this shit got ghost after and did it solo."

"Shit," CJ said with a shake of his head as he rubbed his

hands down his face. I could see this shit was really starting to get to him. I didn't tell him, but I had a feeling this shit ain't have nothing to do with us and everything to do with Dove and her people. We'd been moving smooth with no problems, then that shit with Tika happened. After that people started talking and moving different. But I couldn't put all the blame on CJ, especially since I was under Lily just like he was under Dove. "I gotta figure something out."

"I mean, it maybe something we don't ever know," I said with a shrug of my shoulders as I read my text from Re'Gine. She was already hitting a nigga up for some more dick like I didn't just leave her ass. She even sent a video of her touching on her pussy.

"Nigga, are you listening to me?" CJ questioned. I looked up from my phone with a smile on my face. "Bro, whoever shorty is, go back to her cause you ain't no help right now. Let me know when you ready to put that work in."

"Nigga, I'm here, ain't I?" I questioned with a laugh as I dropped my phone back into my lap. "What else you want from me? I already told you ain't nobody talking. Shit!"

"Don't even worry about it, nigga. I'll figure this shit out on my own," CJ as he picked up the phone and started texting. "I'll catch you around, Benny."

Chapter Twelve

DOVE

"Hello?" I said with an attitude after answering an unknown number. I was in the middle of trying to style my braids down and the number kept calling over and over. After like the seventh time, I finally answered.

"Hey girl," said a voice. I pulled the phone away from my face and stared at it. I knew that voice but hadn't talked to the person on the other end in over a year. "Dove? Dove, you there, girl?"

"Yeah Red, I'm here," I replied as I put the phone on speaker and sat it on the bed. I had about thirty minutes before CJ would be home and I wanted to be ready to talk as soon as he walked in the door.

"Good, I thought I had the wrong number 'cause you wasn't answering," Red said, then let out a deep sigh as if everything was good with us and we talked all the time. "I wanted to tell you I was back in town and wanted to see if you wanted to get together and catch up." If I didn't know any better, I would think that Red was a real friend and was just trying to catch up. But I knew better. Over the last year,

I realized who was really my friend and who wasn't, and Red was in the latter group.

"Red, where you been?" I questioned as I tucked my last braid into my halo and pushed a bobby pin in to help keep the style.

"Girl, I was in Georgia and then Florida. Shit was just too hectic around here for me and I needed a break," Red said. "I been back for a few weeks, just working and taking care of my baby and I told my mama I had to reach out and tell you I was home."

"Baby? You had a baby?" I questioned in surprise. Since I could remember Red said she never wanted kids. Said that they were a big ass problem that she didn't need in her life. So, if she had a baby, it must've been for a reason. "Who the hell did you have a baby by?"

"Girl, that's why I said we gotta catch up," Red said with a laugh. The fact that she didn't answer my question didn't go unnoticed. "Maybe we can meet up near that little Café you like to eat at near Sage's house. Hell, even invite her, too. I know she doesn't really care for me, but I would love for her to see my baby. Maybe she can give me some parenting advice."

"Um Red, Sage passed away about a month ago," I said. I immediately got sad thinking about my sister.

"Girl, what?!" Red questioned. "What you mean Sage passed away? What happened?"

"Um she was killed in a drive-by shooting," I said as I wiped tears from my face.

"Oh girl, I'm so sorry. How is your family holding up?" Red asked. Her concern sounded sincere, but I'd known Red long enough to know to never take anything at face value. "Have y'all found out who did it yet?"

"Not yet. But CJ, Benny, Bleus and Trigga are looking into it." I picked up my phone and logged onto the security camera feed and watched the garage door open. "Let me call you back Red, CJ just pulled up and I need to talk to him about something."

"Okay girl, don't forget to call me back," Red said just as I hung up.

I jumped from the bed and made my way downstairs. I stepped into the kitchen at the same time that CJ opened the door. I could feel my heart beating so fast that I thought, at any moment, it could jump out of my chest.

"Hey," I said just above a whisper. CJ closed the door and dropped his keys onto the counter. He crossed his arms over his chest and stared down at me. "I, um, well." I took a deep breath and tried to get myself together. "I wanted to talk to you." Because CJ was so stubborn, I didn't think he would start talking first. If anything, I knew he would wait me out. Even though he gave me a deadline on when I would have to have my ass home.

"Come here," CJ said. He hadn't moved from next to the back door, but without hesitation I did what he asked. I looked up at him as I stood in front of him. I wanted to reach up and grab him, but the look on his face told me not to press my luck. "Say what you gotta say, Dove. I'm too tired to pretend to know what you're thinking. You were Billy Bad Ass when I was at your mama's house, so you gotta have that same energy now. Except don't holler at me, my patience is too short for that shit right now."

"I wanted to tell you I was sorry," I said with a shaky voice as I rubbed my hands together. "I realized how out of line I was with you and I'm sorry for that. You have been nothing but supportive through everything, and as your woman I should have given you the respect that you deserve."

"Yeah mama, you been trippin' hard as of lately," CJ said with a laugh as he wiped his hands down his face. "Look, I get you going through it 'cause of your sister's death. I mean, I haven't had to bury a sibling or nothing, but I understand you in pain."

"But you didn't deserve to be treated the way you were."

"Nah I didn't, so let that be the last time you ever trip out on me like that again," CJ said with a smirk on his face as he closed the little distance between us. "You carrying my seed in there, he gonna know who run this shit and it ain't his mama."

"CJ, you don't know if it's a boy or not," I said with a laugh as he lifted my shirt over my head.

"Mama, this is a boy in there growing," CJ said as he palmed my stomach with his hand. Even though I was only four months along and didn't look pregnant to anyone who didn't know me, I knew CJ could tell. My stomach had a small pudge to it but was hard. Every day I found myself touching it, amazed that I was going to be somebody's mama. "Let's make a deal, if it's a girl you can name her. But if it's a boy, then I get to name him."

"Deal," I said with a smile. "I have a doctor's appointment in a few weeks and we can find out the gender then. And let's put it out there right now, no naming the baby after us. There will be no Clever III or Dove Junior running around here."

Instead of responding, CJ nodded his head and bent down so he was eye level with my stomach. He rested his head against me and spoke to our baby in a soft voice that even I couldn't hear. "Alright my man, remember what I said. Daddy loves you, but this shit gotta be done, okay?"

"CJ, what did you say to my baby?" I questioned with a laugh as he stood.

"That's between me and my son," he said with another smile on his face as he began to trace the lining of my bra. "You gonna have to learn to let us get our time in, he not gonna want to hang out with you every day. You already got an advantage 'cause you carrying him for nine months. But after that, he's gonna be my rider, watch what I tell you."

"CJ?" I said with a shaky voice as he cupped my breast. We hadn't had sex in almost two months, and I was horny as hell. So his touch was doing things to my body that damn near had be cumming. "Baby, I don't care what you and the baby talked about because right now I need you inside me."

Before I could say anything else, he spun me around and I braced my hands on the wall that was next to me. I heard his shorts drop to the ground then he reached around and grabbed my throat. Bending my neck so I could see him, he kissed me. I moaned as soon as our lips touched. Normally, CJ was a gently lover, never being too rough, he made sure I enjoyed every touch, lick, and feel. But this was different. His touch wasn't rushed but it was forceful, and I loved it.

CJ finally pulled back from the kiss, but only to start kissing down the side of my neck, then biting me. He wrapped his arms around me just in time, because my knees gave out.

"Open your legs more."

I did as I was told and spread my legs. CJ reached down and pulled my shorts down. I smiled when I heard him groan and say, "You knew your ass was going to be bent over somewhere in this house. That's why yo' ass ain't got no panties on." He smacked my ass then kissed the sting away. Because of our height difference when he stood, his dick was poking me in the small of my back and the heaviness of his dick had my pussy dripping even more.

"Bend your ass over, and you better not run from me, either."

I braced my hands further apart on the wall and did what I was told. CJ squatted down then lined his dick up with my pussy and pushed himself in. I dropped my head down and moaned in pleasure as he filled me up inch by inch.

"I told my son that I was about to fuck the shit out his mama and he would have to forgive me, but we both need this," CJ said then he started to move in and out of me. "You talked all that big shit in front of your people, and you know how I get down," CJ said. I moved my body closer to the wall and CJ moved his body right with mine. There was no escaping him, and to be honest, I didn't want to, either. "I love you, Dove. Do you hear me?" CJ reached around and gripped the front of my throat, applying enough pressure to heighten my pleasure but not enough to hurt me. "I asked you a question, Dove."

"Yes CJ, I hear you," I replied as he smacked my ass. I bite into my bottom lip to keep my moan at bay. I knew without a doubt that it would annoy CJ because he loved to hear me moan, but I wanted to show him that he wasn't completely in control.

"Stop playing with me then," CJ said. He let my neck go and reached around to pinch my nipples which added the little bit of pain I enjoyed with sex.

"Fuck!" I said as I felt my first orgasm start to build. It didn't take long because CJ was hitting my favorite spot over and over. "CJ, baby, I'm about to cum already."

"Nah, don't do that, baby," CJ said as he slowed down his pace but still hit my spot. "You can't already be ready to cum just yet. I ain't even been in you that long."

"But, oooh! Damn, CJ. I can't stop it," I moaned. I could feel my legs starting to shake and my breathing started to quicken.

"Then give me my nut, Dove," CJ whispered into my ear just before he bit it. I balled up my fist and beat it into the wall as my orgasm rolled through me. "You about to have a long ass night, 'cause I ain't been in your pussy for a while and I got a lot of time to make up for." CJ pulled out of me and spun me around. I looked down and realized he was still hard after already coming.

"I love you, Clever," I said as he bent down to help me out of my shorts.

"I love you, too, Dove," CJ said with a laugh as he looked up at me. "Now move your ass, 'cause I'm about to fuck you until you pass out."

I happily did as I was told.

"What do you mean you think Benny moving funny?" I asked CJ the next morning as we stood in the kitchen making breakfast. We'd spent most of the night fucking. We only stopped when my stomach started to cramp up. We ended up showering and falling asleep as soon as our heads hit the pillow.

"He just moving different is all," CJ said with a shrug of his shoulders as I glanced over at him. I moved around him to get the mushrooms out the fridge and waited for him to explain in more detail what he meant.

"CJ, I need more than that," I said with a laugh.

"Mama, nigga is just different is all. I can't really explain it, but the shit don't sit right with me."

"Has he said something? Money not adding up? Story don't check out?" I questioned as I sliced up the mushrooms and dumbed them into a bowl. "I mean, I know men are different than woman when it comes to watching for shit, but you've known Benny pretty much your entire life. You would know if something isn't right."

"Nah money is good, but he been messing with this new girl every few weeks and now he late to meetings, if he even shows up. Don't answer the phone when I call. It's like he don't care about the business shit no more, and is only worried about getting his dick wet."

"CJ, that man ain't moving funny," I said with another laugh. "He's just moving different in his life than you are. You're settled down with a woman and kid on the way. He's living the bachelor life and enjoying it. When he was with Lily, y'all were doing the same things, now you're not. That doesn't mean he's moving different."

"The man moving different," CJ said with a little too much conviction. It was like he knew something I didn't and instead of just outright saying it, he was beating around the bush with bullshit. "Like this nigga was three hours late to our meeting last night because he was messing around with a new chick named Re'Gine."

"You mean Regina?" I questioned.

"Nah Re'Gine, like that 90's Sitcom character, the one with Queen Latifa?" CJ questioned like he was trying to remember the show.

"You mean Livin' Single?" I answered him. I sat down the knife and turned to face him. CJ stood against the fridge with his arms crossed deep in thought. "The character's name was Re'Gine, she was played by Kim Fields."

"Yeah, that's the name he said," CJ said with a shake of his head. "Nigga couldn't keep his head out his phone for two seconds to even hold a conversation."

"Baby, I'm sure it's nothing," I said not really paying attention to what CJ was talking about. My mind was racing with ten thousand different thoughts. The main one being Red. Back in the day, she would tell dudes that she really wasn't interested in but was using them that her name was Re'Gine. Plus, the fact that she'd called me yesterday letting me know she was back in town just didn't sit right with me.

"Dove, are you listening to me?" CJ questioned. I pulled

myself out my thoughts and looked up at him. "What you over there thinking about?"

"Yeah, I'm listening," I said. I sat down the knife I had in my hand on the counter and walked over to him. "And I was thinking about sucking your dick until your toes curl, if that's okay with you."

"Hell yeah it's okay," CJ said with a smile. As I dropped down to my knees, I pulled his already hard dick out of his basketball shorts. "If you gonna suck my dick, Dove, suck it." I licked the tip of CJ's dick before I deep-throated him. "Fuck yeah baby, do the damn thing."

Chapter Thirteen

CJ

"Nigga, if you don't tell me what the fuck you know so I can go," I said as I propped my feet up on an expensive ass chair in Mickey's office.

I looked over at Mickey and hoped and prayed this nigga didn't go off the deep end and just shoot up the place. We'd been in a meeting to discuss me purchasing another business when his secretary Shelly came barging into his office to tell him some man was outside claiming to be his brother-in-law. Since I was in his office, Mickey had no idea who Shelly was talking about and was about to tell her that whoever was outside would have to wait. Then Memphis walked in, and it took everything in me to hold Mickey back, because he was out for blood.

"Yo' ass ain't got nowhere to be," Memphis said, waving me off. I wanted to deny it, but the shit was true. Dove was with her mama and sister spending some quality time together, and wouldn't be ready for me to pick her up for another three hours. "You rushing me like my sisters ain't busy, so that's why you niggas spending quality time together.

Doing the whole brother-in-law thing and didn't think to invite me."

"The fuck we need to invite you for?" Mickey said with a humorless laugh. "Last time I checked, you threatened to kill my wife when you saw her last."

"I threaten to kill everybody that pisses me off, Mickey Mouse. Chill out, nigga. I called Falcon like three days later and apologized," Memphis said with a shrug of his shoulders as he continued to break down his weed. "Ain't my fault y'all don't know how to let shit go."

"First off nigga, don't call me no fucking Mickey Mouse. Respect my name or don't say shit to me," Mickey said. I could see the vein in the middle of his forehead start to stick out. This nigga really hated Memphis and was trying his hardest to control his temper. "Second, my wife said you called her laughing about the shit, like it was a damn joke. How the fuck you apologize for threatening to blow your sister brains out? 'Cause to me, that shit don't sound right?"

"Nigga, I didn't threaten my sister's life. I threatened yours," Memphis said. He stopped and looked over at us with a smirk on his face before he went back to finishing up rolling his blunt. I glanced back over at Mickey who sat there dumbfounded. What the fuck was Memphis threatening Mickey for? From what I'd heard about him, he wasn't the normal big brother who was protective of his sisters. Everybody said he hated them 'cause his mama and Rose beefed hard.

"Nigga, what the fuck are you talking about?" Mickey said with a shake of his head. "I'd never met your crazy ass before then."

"I came by doing my nightly sweep of they block one night and saw you and Falcon kicking it," Memphis said before he lit his blunt. "At first I let that shit pass 'cause you was a nerdy-looking nigga back in the day. Then I was talking to my homeboy that I kept posted on they block, and he let me know you was trying to be her nigga. Again, I didn't think twice about it 'cause you didn't look like Falcon's type. But then yo' ass started beefing up."

"So, you threatened my life?" Mickey questioned with a raised eyebrow. I let out a little laugh but didn't say anything as they went back and forth. The shit was obvious to me. Memphis took his job as big brother serious, even though he didn't let it be known. It wouldn't have mattered who his sisters would've ended up with back in the day, Memphis would've threatened whoever, and more than likely did with the other sisters.

"Yep," Memphis said with a nod. He took a long pull of his blunt and continued to nod his head. It was almost like he was having a conversation with himself and we were just waiting on him to finish.

"How many other of the sister's boyfriends did you threaten?" I questioned as I adjusted my shirt.

"All of them," Memphis replied. "I had Bleus checked at gun point. Crazy ass nigga laughed in my face and told me he would gladly be Sage's man if she let him. Lily little nigga told me a price and he would disappear, but that was after I'd just got back in town and she'd lost the baby. I beat that nigga within an inch of his life and let him heal only to do it over and over again for about six months. But he finally got the picture. If I'd known he was hitting her, I would've gladly killed him."

"Why didn't you?" I questioned.

"That nigga Bleus and his homebody took care of it."

"So, then you threatened me?" Mickey questioned as he typed at his computer. Since we'd been here Mickey would pull up different files and work over them while we talked. He said it was better to channel is anger and direct it at making money than putting a bullet in whoever pissed him off. And right now, the person who was pissing him off was Memphis.

"Consider yourself lucky, you were the first nigga I threatened. I had mad respect for you back in the day 'cause you wasn't scared," Memphis said as he tried to pass me his blunt. I shook my head and pulled out my own. The only person I shared a blunt with was my woman and she wasn't smoking anytime soon. "Check it CJ, this little nigga was coming out the gym and me and my boy rolled up. We called him out and let him know to leave Falcon alone. This fool laughed at us and said he was on his way home to have my sister suck his dick." Memphis took another pull of his blunt, held the smoke in for a few seconds, then blew it out. "Of course, I snapped. I was going off so much I didn't realize Falcon had walked up on us. I was really pointing at that nigga yelling, talking about I would kill him. Shit, I was so far gone it was crazy. When my homeboy told me a few days later that I'd threatened Falcon too, I called her up to apologize. I was laughing 'cause I legit thought it was funny that I didn't remember seeing her."

"Let me guess, Falcon didn't find shit funny about it and went off?" I said.

"Baby sis threatened to kill me over Mickey Mouse. Told me straight out if she had to prove her loyalty that I shouldn't second-guess that she was going to ride for her nigga."

"She told that nigga she would put a bullet between his eyes and sleep peacefully about it," Mickey said with a smile. Falcon was a true rider when it came to him, so there wasn't a doubt in my mind she would kill Memphis without a second thought.

"And it ain't a doubt in my soul that she would do it, too," Memphis said with a smirk on his face. This nigga got a kick out of fucking with people. It didn't matter if you were family or not, he was going to get into your head and enjoyed every minute of it. "Which is why I always have my piece ready when I see her."

"Nigga, you full of shit," I said with a laugh. I pulled my phone from my pocket to check my messages. I'd hit up Benny a few hours ago, letting him know we need to link up for some work. But in typical Benny fashion as of late, he hadn't hit me back yet. "It's one thing to beef with them, but I highly doubt you'd pull your gun, let alone shot one of them. Plus, if you did we'd go to war over they asses in a minute."

"Which I respect," Memphis said. He pulled his own phone from his pocket and read his text messages. Whatever he read must have been something he didn't want to 'cause his face twisted up in disgust before he threw it on the table. "But this shit with Sage is heavy on my heart. I always thought I would have time to fix my mistakes with them. I know our pops wasn't shit. He treated our moms like trash and then that shit he pulled with Rose? Man, that shit was foul as hell. Especially 'cause she held his ass down."

"Did you know he was keeping tabs on Dove through her ex?" I questioned. Tika was the type of nigga that didn't pay attention to what he said when he was mad. He'd spilled different information each time I saw him. The main thing being that Mister owed him and he planned to collect with a baby from Dove.

"I heard," Memphis said. He reached down and picked his vibrating phone back up. Whoever was texting him must have really needed or wanted to get his attention, but why they didn't just call him was beyond me. "Look, I know they think I'm like Mister, but I definitely ain't. That fool did my mama wrong too, and even though she wanted me to ride with that nigga, I just couldn't."

"Then why you let your sisters think you did?" Mickey questioned. His attention was no longer on his computer and fully on Memphis now. "If you ain't like y'all pops, why let them think you were?"

"Shit was for their protection. Mister had too many enemies and didn't give a fuck about nobody but himself. It was better for them to think I was like him than to know I was out there making sure they names never came up in something," Memphis said as he pulled another bag of weed out his pocket and began to break it down. Even with his attention on making sure he got all the seeds and stems out, he was still being one hundred with us. "Even if this stuff with Sage hadn't happened, I was still coming back."

"For what?" I questioned. Again, I checked my phone, hoping to see that Benny had finally hit me back. "Huh? What you come back for, then?

"Redemption. I want them to get to know me," Memphis said looking up at me. "I want them to see I ain't like that nigga. And to understand all that shit I did in the past was to protect them. Now I ain't saying I'm a saint and I'm innocent, but I can say I ain't as bad as they think I am. Yeah, I'm a killer, even slang every once and a while. But shit, so are they and y'all for all that it matters."

"That's true," Mickey said. He sat back in his seat and watched Memphis. We couldn't tell Memphis he was wrong because he wasn't. We'd all done shit that others would consider unforgiveable, but not the people in our lives. They understood the game and the men they chose to be deal with. Not everyone was as lucky as we were. "Now, to let y'all know why I'm here. The person you looking for? Her name is Red."

"Shit!" I said as I dropped my head into my hands. I knew I should've killed that bitch when I had the chance. I had no idea how I was going to tell Dove that her ex-best friend was responsible for her sister's death. There was no way shit could get worse at this point.

"And I'm pretty sure she's fucking with your homeboy Benny," Memphis said. Looks like I was wrong, and shit just got worse.

Chapter Fourteen

DOVE

I stepped out the car, looking around to make sure I could see all possible exits just in case shit didn't feel right. Since the shooting with Tika last year, I didn't ever let my guard down. The only time I had was the BBQ for Mama and then that got shot up. So now I refused to let someone catch me slipping again. Closing the door, I made my way towards the restaurant. Since the lunch rush was over, there weren't too many people left inside.

"Hi my," I stopped midsentence and rethought my statement. Red wasn't someone I considered a friend any longer. The young hostess looked up from her computer and waited for me to continue. "Umm, I have someone waiting on me. She said she was seated in the back, she just texted me." I flashed my phone that was in my hand as if it was some kind of proof. Red had texted me, but since my screen was locked and I had no intention of unlocking it to show her my text, she would just have to take my word for it.

"Yes ma'am, I know who you are talking about. She just flagged me down a few minutes ago to tell me you were on your way," the young lady said as she turned to grab a menu.

"If you don't mind, please follow me." I nodded my head and followed her. For some reason, I was nervous. The thought of seeing Red after all this time had my heart pounding wildly in my chest.

At first, I thought my eyes were playing tricks on me. Instead of seeing the loud blue hair and too tight and flashy clothes, sat a toned-down version of Red. She wore a simple black weave, naturally beat face, no long eyelashes, and from what I could tell her outfit was simple. She looked like the Red that I always envisioned for her to look like if she just let that ghetto girl persona go.

"Dove," Red said with a smile as I sat down. The hostess sat down my menu and took my drink order before letting us know our server would be over shortly. "I'm so glad you agreed to meet me."

"I mean you didn't give me too much of a choice, did you?" I said. I sat my purse in the empty chair next to me. "You called me what? Twenty-two times between last night and this morning?"

"I know, I just really wanted to see you," Red said. "Since we talked, and you told me about Sage, I wanted to make sure you're okay." She sounded genuine with her concern, which I needed. I couldn't stand the fake sympathy that so many people were giving me. "I mean, I know you won't be completely a hundred percent okay, but I wanted you to know that I was heartbroken to hear everything. I ended up calling my mama and asking her why she didn't tell me about Sage. She said that she was respecting y'all family wishes and didn't want me to fly back home and stir up some shit."

"Which is true," I said with a nod. Our server came, dropped off our drinks, and took out order. Even though I wasn't hungry, I knew I could always take the food home and CJ would eat it. Once our server was gone, we continued with our conversation. "We just wanted to mourn in peace. Which is what we are still doing. Then, the fact we have to give Juke some type of new normalcy is stressful, too."

"Oh, I know that baby is just heartbroken right now," Red said with a shake of her head. "I couldn't imagine having to try and explain that to him right now."

"The only plus is that my mama is home," I said with a shrug of my shoulders as I looked around the restaurant. "She's been a major help with him. Majority of the time he's either with her or Bleus."

"Wait, your mom is home?" Red questioned. The look and surprise were evident in her voice. It looked like her mama wasn't telling her shit while she was gone. "When did that happen?"

"A few weeks before Sage's death. They found out some stuff that didn't add up with her case," I replied. I intentionally left out any information about my mama's case. Even though she was home, it didn't mean that she couldn't go back because of some hater. And even though just last year I considered Red my best friend, I couldn't say that right now.

"Damn, that's crazy. I'm going to have to go see her," Red said. I didn't say anything about her comment. Mainly because I knew my mama would more than likely not say a word to Red. She didn't like her, hadn't from the moment she met her. Mama said Red was the type of chick that was only loyal to herself. She'd sell out God if the Devil offered her the right amount money and social media followers.

"Right now, she's focused on Juke," I replied. It was the only thing I could think of to say that wouldn't cause her to feel like I didn't want that. "Give her some time to get him together."

"Of course," Red replied with a smile on her face. As she began to talk, I found myself zoning out. The years Red and I had been friends felt like a million years ago. I couldn't say we'd grown apart because I don't think we were ever on the same level.

"Hey, quick question," I said interrupting her.

"What's up?"

"What was the name we would use back in the day when we weren't interested in the guy?" I questioned. "I was talking to Lily and Tatum the other day and they'd gave some guy a their fake names and for the life of me I couldn't remember what the names were that we used."

"Oh girl, you were Karmen with a K not a C, and I was Re'Gine," Red said with a laugh.

"That's right!" I said laughing along with her. "Let me text Lily right now and tell her. For some reason I just couldn't remember." I pulled my phone from my purse and texted CJ instead.

Me: *Baby where are you?*

CJ: *About to walk out the office and head home. What's up?*

Me: *We gotta talk.*

CJ: *Where you at? I'll come to you.*

Me: *No need I will be home in about thirty.*

CJ: *You sure?*

Me: *Yep. Just found out some information that you need to know.*

CJ: *Alright. Bring your ass on or I'm coming to you.*

Me: *See you soon. Love you.*

CJ: *Alright. Love you too.*

"Damn girl, y'all having a whole conversation now, huh?" Red questioned. I dropped my phone back in my purse and looked up at her.

"Yeah, she was telling me that Juke is giving them a hard time so I'm going to have to cut this short."

I didn't want for her reply as I waved the server down and

asked for a to-go box and paid for my portion on the bill. Back in the day I would have covered it all 'cause Red never had any money, or so she claimed. But not now. She was a grown ass woman and if she couldn't cover her bill, she'd better get back there and bust some suds or suck the person in charge's dick 'cause I wasn't about to help her.

"Oh yeah I get that, babies are picky at times," Red said with a nod of her head as she pulled her own wallet out. She paid for her meal and we headed out of the restaurant together. We walked side-by-side not saying a word until we reached our cars, which were parked next to each other. "Girl, you still be driving them little ass cars."

"Yep," I replied as I unlocked my car door. My car wasn't considered small, but next to her big ass Expedition I could see how she thought that. "I see you finally got rid of the Tahoe."

"Yeah," Red retorted with a head nod as she got inside of her own truck the same time I got into mine. I started my car and rolled down my window when I realized she was still talking. "Call me when you make it home."

"Will do," I countered knowing damn well I had no intention of ever speaking to her again.

It took me less than twenty minutes to get home, but when I pulled into the driveway I was met by two men standing on my front porch. The only indication that they were cops was their police-issued black Charger parked in front of my house and their stance. No matter how hard cops tried to play it off, they couldn't turn off their police demeanor, and even though these two were dressed in plain clothes, the way they stood screamed cop. I parked my truck and got out, eyeing them carefully as I shut the door. One was a black guy, looked to be young, maybe in his early thirties with a toothpick hanging out the side of his mouth. Short, but he looked like he was a gym rat because he was buff as hell. Long face, thin lips, beady eyes and bald head. He looked like the type of dude that took steroids and tried to play it off. As I moved closer to them, I realized the one I thought white was really mixed. He was kind of cute, taller and slimmer than his partner, but still had an intimidating look about him. He had sandy blonde hair, piercing blue eyes, thick lips that were encased with a five o'clock shadow. He had a strong broad nose, and when he smiled at me, it was something about him that looked vaguely familiar I just couldn't put my finger on it. I knew that CJ had few different police on his payroll, but they knew better than to come to our house. Plus, I'd never seen these two before.

"Hello," I said as I made my way towards them. The two officers stopped the conversation they were having between them and turned to face me. "Can I help you with something?"

"Yes, we are looking for a—" The black officer said as he adjusted his toothpick in his mouth. He reached into his shirt pocket and pulled out a small notepad. I waited as he flipped through the pages and finally stopped on what he was looking for. "Yeah, I'm looking for Dove Lincoln."

"That would be me," I said cautiously. "What can I help you with?"

"My name is Detective Peters and this is my partner Detective Holmes," the light-skinned one said, cutting off his partner 'cause I could tell he was about to say something to piss me off. I nodded my head, crossed my arms over my chest, and waited for them to continue. "We were wondering if we could ask you a few questions about your ex, Tika Smith."

"What about him?" I questioned with a raised eyebrow. "I haven't seen of spoken to Tika is over a year."

"You think we could take this inside?" Detective Holmes questioned with an attitude.

"I'm fine right here," I said glancing over at him. It was something about his ass I didn't like, and there was no way I was letting him in my house. He looked like the type that would plant something without a second thought. I learned at an early age to never let police into your space. If he wanted to talk, then we would talk right outside. It was a nice day anyway, so there wasn't any reason to waste it being in the house. "Now, what do you need to know?"

"I know you said you haven't spoken to Tika in over a year. Is there a reason for that?" Detective Holmes questioned. "Word on the street is y'all were going heavy, even talked about getting married, then you were linked to another guy. What's his name?" He looked back down at his notepad as if he was searching for a name. "Oh yeah, Clever Jones. Also known as CJ."

"Okay," was my simple reply. I wasn't about to confirm a thing he said. Detective Holmes must have known that because he let out a humorless laugh and tapped at his notepad but didn't say anything.

"Someone in Tika's life is looking for him, so we are checking in with his last known associates to see if they know anything," Detective Peters said. I tilted my head to the side and stared at him as I tried to figure out who he reminded me of. He must've realized I was staring because he pulled out a pair of dark shades from his pocket and put them on.

"People come up missing every day and y'all worried about Tika?" I said. I wasn't worried about them finding Tika's body. Falcon and Mickey had taken care of it and the gun that I used. I was more curious about who had reported Tika missing. From what I'd heard, no one was concerned about him because he had a history of just leaving when the thought hit him. The last I heard, everyone just thought it was one of those times. Especially after he'd been linked to my shooting. "I would be more worried about missing kids and unsolved murders than I would be about Tika if I were y'all."

"Are you aware that Clever Jones is a suspect in Tika's disappearance? Word on the street is he put a bullet in Tika's head because of you," Detective Holmes questioned. I looked over at Detective Peters who looked at his partner like he wanted to punch him in his face. "Something about retaliation because of the drive-by at your home that left you and your neighbor in the hospital and a few of your neighbors even dead."

"I know for a fact that CJ didn't put a bullet in Tika's head," I said with a laugh. I adjusted my purse and shook my head. "It looks like your sources have it wrong."

"And how do you know that, Ms. Lincoln?" Holmes asked with a raised eyebrow. "If he didn't do it. Who did?"

"Explain to me, Detective Holmes, how did you go from Tika is missing to he's dead?" I questioned. Before he could answer, I noticed CJ car pull up in front of the house. He rolled his window down and stared at the two detectives before he rolled it back up. A small smile formed on my face as I watched his pull into the driveway, and just like the kind of man he was, he took his time getting out the car and making his way towards me.

"What's up, baby?" CJ greeted me as he pulled me into a quick hug and kissed me on the forehead. "Can I help you gentlemen?"

"No," Detective Holmes said with a shake of his head. He put his notepad back into his pocket and took off towards his car without another word.

"Good to see you too, Detective Holmes," CJ yelled out to him. I shook my head and turned my attention back to Detective Peters, who still was standing in his spot with his hands in his pocket. "What can I do for you, Detective Peters?"

"Nothing at all, CJ," Detective Peters said with a shake of his head. He followed his partner, only slowing his pace as he neared CJ. "Be careful, he's like a dog on the hunt. Someone is feeding him information and I haven't figured out who it is yet. But he swears he's going to have you locked up by the end of the month. Close in your ranks and clean house."

CJ didn't react verbally to Detective Peters' mumbled words, but I saw his jaw clench a little before he grabbed my hand, and we went into the house.

Chapter Fifteen

CJ

"You gonna tell me what's going on?" Dove questioned as we made our way towards our bedroom.

I nodded my head but didn't say anything yet. Peters' words were racing through my head. Someone was running they damn mouth, and I had a feeling I knew who it was. Crazy shit was it was breaking my heart, because if I was right, I was going to have to put a bullet in Benny's head and I didn't want to do that to the man I considered my brother. But if he'd betrayed me, I had no other choice. "That one Detective work for you or something?"

"What did they say to you before I pulled up?" I questioned. I pulled my shirt over my head as I walked into the closet. I threw it into the clothes hamper, never stopping my movement as I made my way towards the back of it.

"They questioned me about Tika's disappearance. The bald one did majority of the talking," Dove replied from behind me. I glanced over my shoulder to see her standing in the doorframe with her arms crossed. She was starting to show, and that shit did something to me. To see my seed starting to change her body gave me a type of pride I didn't know I would ever feel. "They said someone reported Tika missing, and they were looking into it. But then they changed it up and said that you were a person of interest in his murder. That it was a rumor around town that you put a bullet in his head."

"Well, we both know that isn't true, so I ain't worried about that," I said turning back around. I pushed clothes and boxes out the way from the corner of the closet and kneeled to pull back the floorboard. When I had the house built, I had several fake floorboards installed in almost every room. Majority of them were empty because, before Dove and I got together, I never used this house, so I didn't stash anything in them. "If anything, they are grasping at straws trying to connect the little shit they think they have together."

"But what about what the light-skinned cop said when he walked past us," Dove asked.

"He's just giving me a heads-up on some shit I was already figuring out," I said as I pulled six bands out and sat them next to me. "Look, shit is about to get crazy around here if I'm right about some stuff. So I need you to grab yo' mama, sisters, and nephew, and go on a vacation." I grabbed two guns and closed the floorboard back up.

"CJ, you already know that's not about to happen," Dove said. I could hear the irritation in her voice before I even turned around to face her. Baby was a rider and I loved that about her, but I didn't need her or my child in danger because she was being stubborn. "Plus, I need to tell you what I found out today."

"Dove, listen to me," I said as I made my way to her. "I need you to not fight with me on this. I'm not going to be able to take care of what I need to if I don't know you are safe. You and this baby mean the world to me and this shit I'm about to do—" I stopped talking and palmed her stomach. The thought of Benny betraying me was horrible, but if something happened to Dove and this baby I wouldn't be able to survive. "Baby, just do this for me."

Dove opened her mouth to respond but I kissed her before she could. I put all my energy into the kiss. Telling her without using my words how much she meant to me, because I couldn't verbally bare my soul to her. I pulled back long enough to pull her shirt over her head. I smiled down at her as I directed her to walk backwards and sat her down on the edge of the bed when we reached it.

"CJ, what I have to tell you is important," Dove said. I nodded, dropped to my knees, spread her legs apart, and pushed her long flowy dress up. "You can't just shut me up with some head and dick and think I'm going to do what you say."

"Dove, lay back," I said, looking up at her. I laughed a little when she rolled her eyes but did what I asked. "Damn shame you got on panties 'cause this is another pair you just lost." I ripped her panties in half and went to work at eating her pussy. Dove had the kind of pussy that made me what to stay between her legs all day. The way she responded to my licks, pulls, tugs, and even soft nips at her clit was some of the sexiest shit I'd ever seen. I threw her legs over my shoulders and wrapped my arms around her, anchoring her to the bed. I pulled her clit into my mouth and sucked as Dove moaned loudly.

"CJ baby, that feels so good," Dove moaned. She arched her back off the bed and grabbed her titties. Her eyes rolled in the back of her head and she tossed her head from side-to-side. "CJ!"

"You want me to stop?" I questioned after I let her clit go. I inserted my middle two fingers into her pussy and moved them in and out while I used my thumb to circle her clit. "If you want me to stop, I will baby."

"No CJ, don't stop," Dove panted. "God, please don't stop."

"You sure?" I said as I moved my hand faster. I reached up with my other hand and palmed one of her titties. I tweaked her nipple through the fabric of her bra which had her arching off the bed harder. I could feel her pussy starting to tighten up on my fingers, so I knew that her orgasm was near.

"No! Don't stop CJ, please don't stop," Dove cried out.

"Okay baby, I won't stop," I said as I pulled my hand from her breast. I dropped my shorts and underwear. I was already hard from eating her pussy. "But I can't let you nut on my hand, baby. Nah, you gotta nut all over my dick this time." I pulled my hand back from her pussy, lined myself up to her hole and pushed in slowly. "Shit Dove, you so fucking hot and wet, baby." I braced my hands on the sides of her face and dropped my head down. I gave myself a few seconds to get adjusted to her because if I didn't, I would have busted my nut before I wanted to.

"CJ baby," Dove said as she gripped my face with her hands. "I need you, baby."

I opened my eyes and looked down at Dove. She stared up at me with hooded eyes full of lust. I nodded and slowly started to work my hips back and forth. With each stroke, Dove moaned louder and louder. She let go of my face and gripped my neck, which only caused me to move more. The first time she'd grabbed my head during sex and squeezed I'd nutted harder than I'd did in the past. I could feel her pussy start to throb against my dick.

"You 'bout to cum, baby?" I questioned as I bent down to kiss her quickly. Pulling back, I bit into her, then let it go. "You want me to tell you cum?" She nodded her head as she sucked her lip into her mouth. "You gonna be a good girl if I let you come?" Again, she nodded her head, but I didn't believe her for one second. Her pussy felt too good to argue with her, so I sped up and pulled a hard orgasm from her. I looked down at her pussy as she squirted and moved my hips even faster, this time chasing my own nut.

"Shit," I said as I bent and rested my head on her stomach. "Each time we have sex, I think you pull more nut out of me. I swear if you weren't already pregnant, you would be by the load I just shot into you." I kissed her stomach then unwrapped her legs from around my waist and pulled out of her slowly. "Stay there, I'll let you a towel." I cleaned myself up in the bathroom then made my way back into the room to clean up Dove. She was still in same spot that I'd left her in, only difference now was she had her arms draped over her eyes.

"CJ, I had lunch with Red today," Dove said as I wiped her clean. I stopped moving and looked down at her. She moved her arm from over her face, raised up, and looked at me.

"Why the hell would you do that?" I said with an attitude. I took a step back and just stared at her. "Hell, why didn't I know she got in contact with you until now? Did you forget that bitch had something to do with you being shot?"

"Of course not! But I needed to find out something before I told you," Dove said with a shake of her head as she got out the bed. She pulled her skirt and the little pieces of her panties that were left off and made her way to the dresser. Dove pulled a pair of black yoga pants and matching top out the drawer and put them on.

"What did you need to find out that was so important that you didn't tell me you were meeting up with the bitch you thought was your best friend wasn't really?" I questioned. I picked up all our clothes off the floor and went back to the closet. I tossed them in the same basket I'd thrown my shirt into earlier. I tossed the pieces of her panties into the trash can as I came out. Dove never took her eyes off me as I came out. She watched my semi hard dick sway side-to-side as I moved around. “Stop looking at my dick and tell me.”

“Put some damn underwear on then!” Dove snapped. I pulled open the drawer that I kept my boxer briefs in and pulled a pair on. “Thank you. Okay I know you probably know that females will use a fake name when they are out, and they meet a guy that aren’t interested in.” I nodded my head and crossed my arms over my chest waiting for her to get to her point. “So back in the day when Red and I would go out, we had our secret names already picked. We didn’t mix it up ‘cause that’s how females got caught. If you stuck with one name then it was easier to remember when you or your homegirl got drunk. Well anyway, I went by Karmen. Guess what Red went by?”

“What does this have to do with anything, Dove?” I questioned.

“You said that Benny was acting funny, right?” Dove answered.

“Right,” I nodded. I went back to the closet for two reasons. One I needed clothes, and two I didn’t want Dove to see my face when she dropped what she knew on me. The second she saw my face, she would know that I already knew what she was about to tell me.

“You also said Benny is messing with a new chick named Re’Gine,” Dove said. “Well back in the day Red’s other name was Re’Gine. I think Benny is messing with Red.”

“I already know, Dove,” I said as I made my way out the closet already dressed in all-black. “Memphis told me and Mickey the other day. Which is why I need you and your sisters to get out of town. I got a funny feeling I’m about to go to war with my brother.”

Chapter Sixteen

BENNY

"Man, I didn't know you were here waiting," I yelled out to Trigga's receding back as I pulled my office door closed with Re'Gine's hand in mine.

He threw up his hand in acknowledgement but didn't say anything. I'd left to make a food run and ran into Re'Gine. Even though I knew I shouldn't 'cause I had shit to do, I ended up bringing her back to the club and letting her suck my dick in my office. I knew Trigga was on his way after running over to Ms. Clever's house to check on Tiny. We'd both been waiting on Bleus and CJ to finally make their appearance, but they hadn't shown up yet. I was mentally preparing to clown CJ 'cause, as of late, he was on my ass about being late and now it was him who was running behind.

"Give me a second and I'll meet you at the pool table."

I pulled Re'Gine behind me and we made our way to the back where she parked her car.

"Aye, I'mma hit you later up tonight so we can link up," I said as pulled open the door of her Expedition after she unlocked the door. "I don't know what time this meeting is going to be done, but I ain't done with your sexy ass yet."

"Who was that guy in their earlier? Is that your partner?' Re'Gine questioned as she looked back the building.

"Nah, that's Trigga," I said with a shake of my head. I closed the door after she started the car and rolled down the windows. "He's just one of my homeboys."

"You gonna really call me or play me off like last time?" Re'Gine questioned with a pout on her face. I reached up, cupped her chin, pulling her face towards mine, and kissed her.

"Nah baby, I'm gonna hit you up as soon as I'm done here. I don't want to hear nothing if it's late either, 'cause it might be," I said letting her face go.

"It's gonna be some bitches here?" Re'Gine questioned. "'Cause I swear I'll come up here and show out."

"You acting like you my girl or something," I said with a laugh as I rubbed my hand over my head. The death stare that she gave me made me laugh harder. For the past few weeks, she'd been hinting at wanting to put a title on what we were doing, but I wasn't ready for all that. I learned my lesson with Lily and rushing things. What Re'Gine and I were doing was cool for now and I was good with where we were at. "But ain't no females gonna be up here, except maybe CJ's woman Dove and Mickey's wife Falcon. That's it."

"Alright Benny," Re'Gine said as she put her truck in reverse and pulled off. I watched as she pulled out the driveway and two cars pulled in. I knew Mickey's truck, but the other one I'd never seen before. Mickey got out the car, rounded it, and opened the passenger door for Falcon, who stepped out. She didn't take her eyes off the other car as she took Mickey's hand and walked towards me.

"What's up, y'all?" I spoke. Mickey nodded his head, but Falcon didn't say anything. I was used to her on and off attitude, so I didn't offend me that she didn't say anything. "Whose car is that?" I nodded my head in the direction of the other car just as the doors opened. Out stepped a tall dark-skinned nigga with a fade in a pair of orange shorts, black shirt, and black and orange Nike's. The woman with him looked familiar as hell. Shorty was yellow, round face, thick lips, and small ass nose freckles running across it. As they moved closer, I could see she had bright green eyes. She wore some grey jogger pants, a black tank top, and a pair of Jordan silver toe Retro High OG's.

"You better not try and shoot this nigga either, Falcon," I heard Mickey say next to me. I turned my attention back to them and watched as Falcon simply looked at Mickey and slowly blinked before turning to head into the building. "Fucking woman so trigger happy."

"You married her crazy ass," I said with a laugh. "Can't be mad at her for doing what she always does."

"I didn't ask your ass shit, Benny," Mickey said with an attitude.

"What's up, Mickey," ole boy said as he stood in front of us. He smiled at us like he knew a secret we didn't. The woman he was with just stared at us, kind of reminded me of Falcon with her stand-offish attitude. "How you doing, man?"

"If you make me regret you being around her, I'm going to kill you my damn self," Mickey said pulling the man into a quick hug and nodding his head at the woman. "Get your boy now, 'cause I can already tell he about to be on some shit."

"I can't control him any better than you can his sister," shorty said with a laugh. "At this point, we just gonna have to put them in a room together and wait to see who comes out living."

"My money is on my wife," Mickey said with a laugh. "Anyway, Benny this is the oldest Lincoln sibling Memphis. Memphis, this is Benny, CJ's right hand and Lily's ex." Memphis looked over at the woman he was with, nodded his head, and they went inside the building without saying a word.

"What the fuck is up with that nigga?" I questioned Mickey. I turned my attention to front gate as it opened again. This time CJ pulled in. He parked his car, got out, and just like Mickey, he wasted no time going to open the door for Dove. They made their way over to us, stopping to greet Mickey and me.

"What's good, my nigga?" I said to CJ as I pulled him into a hug. I nodded over at Dove when he let me go, but that was it. Since the shit with Lily and then Sage's death, I steered clear of Dove as much as possible.

"Man, not shit. Everybody here?" CJ said as he pulled Dove closer to him.

"Everybody but Bleus," I replied.

"He will be here in a little, I just talked to him," CJ said with a nod of his head. "He just dropped Juke off with Ms. Rose."

"That's cool, let's head in 'cause I got a feeling my wife about to go off on this nigga Memphis by now," Mickey said.

We followed him without a second thought. We found everybody in the conference room. Falcon stood near the window with her arms crossed. I could tell from the way her foot was tapping that she was close to going off. Memphis, and the woman he came with, stood at the table while Trigga sat across from them looking mad as hell. Just as we sat down, Bleus walked in. He greeted the room and took his seat next to Trigga. He looked over at Trigga, then the woman with Memphis, and laughed.

"Aye, you serious right now?" Bleus questioned looking over at CJ, who just nodded his head and laughed. "Nigga, that shit is too crazy. After all this shit over little mama, I want to talk to you, 'cause I got mad respect for your ass."

"Ain't nobody talking to her ass but me," Trigga said with a head shake. "Baby talked too much shit that day. Ain't no running this time." His comment only made CJ, Memphis, and Bleus laugh harder. Whatever the inside joke was between the room meant nothing to me.

"Nigga, Golden don't spook easily, so keep that tough shit to yourself," Memphis said, still laughing. "But let's get down to business. I got other shit to handle after this."

"Alright so look, I think I brought everybody here 'cause with the help of Memphis, we were able to find out who is responsible for Sage's death," CJ said. He looked over at Dove, who stood next to Falcon, who had her arms wrapped around her.

"So who did that shit, so we can go take care of them," I said. I was ready for some action, and even though I kept my distance from her sisters I wanted justice just like they did. Sage was an innocent bystander and if they knew who it was, then I was ready to pop some shit off. "CJ, who did this shit nigga?"

"You really about to play dumb, nigga?" Memphis questioned. I looked over at him, confused as hell as to why he was talking to me. "Ain't you the one messing with Red?"

"Red?" I asked still confused. "You talking about Dove old friend? I ain't never met that bitch a day in my life, let alone fucking around with her."

"She was at the party Tika threw at this club last year for Dove," Falcon said. "Tall, brown, blue hair, long lashes, and nails. Sound familiar?"

"No," I said with a shake of my head. "It was so much shit going on when CJ and I rolled up, I don't remember no damn girl. My only focus was getting out that shit alive and then getting your car to CJ house afterwards."

"Nigga, you been messing around with her for a few weeks," Bleus said from his spot. He looked like he was ready to jump across the table and square-up with a nigga. "You trying to tell me you ain't know it was her?"

"Hell yeah, that's what I'm telling you!" I said as I jumped up from my seat.

"She toned down her looks. Re'Gine is really Red," Dove said. My mind was racing with thoughts. *How was I going to know that Red and Re'Gine was the same person?* That night when everything went down at the club, I was so hyped I wasn't worried about no bitch. And when we moved Dove into CJ's spot, she didn't have any pictures up of her, just ones of her family. So, there was no way I'd ever seen her.

"You know how many bitches I've fucked with in the last few months? I don't keep them around longer than a month, and when we link it its always at a hotel or they spot. CJ, do you believe this shit, man?" I said, looking over at CJ who just sat there with head down. "CJ, nigga you believing this shit, too? After all the shit we been through, you believe I would turn on you? What the fuck do I have to gain by killing Sage?"

"That's what I want to know, Benny," CJ said as he raised his head to look up at me.

I could see the pain in his eyes, my boy was torn. He wanted to believe me, I could tell, but he had to look at it from all angles. I was bitter about the fact that Lily had left me. I blamed her sisters for the shit, even though him and Mickey tried to warm me. I just didn't want to listen. I knew I fucked up hitting up Carter that day, but I wasn't lying to her. If I could do it all over again, I would've chose Carter. I would've made her my wife and had about three or four kids by now. I wouldn't be in these streets doing shit I knew I had no business doing.

But the fast money kept calling my name and CJ and I were trying to go clean. He was just doing a better job of it, because he wanted to live that straight life for Dove and his grandma, who begged him on a daily to straighten up. After Lily finally let a nigga know she was really done, I was fucking around with any and every woman that passed by me. Then his house was shot up, killing his girl's sister and putting his entire family in danger. I pulled back from him and his new family. Looking back at it now, I could see how jealous I was of the shit. I mean yeah, I was helping him look. But again, I was more worried about myself and keeping my dick wet.

"Tell me yo' side of it, 'cause my nigga that shit don't look good for you."

"I just met that bitch at Carter's restaurant a while back," I said looking around the table. "It was after Sage was killed. Matter of fact, it was after the Focus concert. She walked up to me spitting her little game or whatever and I swooped her ass up."

"But you been kicking it with her ever since, right?" Falcon asked. She and Dove sat down next to CJ at the table. I could tell from their facial expression that they didn't believe a damn thing I said. "Yo' ass been chopping it up with that hoe for about a month. You trying to tell me you weren't pillow talking?"

"I don't pillow talk with hoes! We fucked, that's it! They don't be around long enough to know shit about me but my name. They don't know where I live, work, none of that shit 'cause I don't bring them around none of that." I responded. I could feel the vein in my neck start to bulge out, which was a sure sign I was getting upset. "Look, I ain't a nigga who loyalty you gotta question. I been by CJ side damn near our entire lives. Ain't been one time that nigga had to question me. Now 'cause y'all see me with a bitch that been had it in for Dove, y'all want to blame that shit on me? So how much sense does that make? That bitch was fucking with her nigga the entire time they was together."

"He couldn't have been the one who set y'all up in the

first place," Memphis said with a shake of his head as he looked through his phone. "Nigga been chasing behind her for a month. Sis been gone longer than that."

"Exactly what I'm trying to tell y'all!" I said. I threw my hands up in frustration and dropped back into my seat.

"That don't mean you ain't telling her shit now, though," Memphis said. He handed his phone to the phone to the woman he was with. She looked it over then handed it back to him.

"What the fuck I gotta do to prove this shit to y'all?" I said. I wasn't a begging type of nigga, but I wasn't about to go out like this either. If they were going to kill me, it was going to be because I did something, not because they thought I was pillow talking with some bitch and set up people that I considered family.

"Call that bitch, tell her to meet up with you, and we can figure all this shit out," Bleus said. He swung his chair side-to-side, looking pissed as hell, and rightfully so. Right now, it looked like I took the woman he loved from her position right next to him and put her in the ground. If I was him, I would've shot first and never asked questions. "But let me tell you something Benny, if you lying I'm going to put your entire family in the ground without a second thought. Do you understand me?"

"Yeah nigga, I got you," I said as I pulled out my phone and dialed Red's number. I put it on speaker just so they didn't think I was hiding something.

"Hey baby," Red said after picking up the phone. "Let me step outside real quick, these kids running around here being all loud and shit. My sister hyped them up on candy then dropped them off to my mama. Ole scandalous ass hoe." As she talked the loudness in the background started to fade away. "Your meeting already over with?"

"Yeah, we wrapping this shit up now," I said looking

around the room. My eyes stopped on Dove before bouncing over to CJ, whose focus was on the window. I could tell he was still listening to the conversation even though he wasn't looking over at the phone.

"You ready for another round? That shit I did to you in your office earlier got you calling me back quick as hell," Red said. I laughed at her comment but inwardly cringed. I just told these niggas I didn't have her around my personal space. Shit had honestly slipped my mind until she brought it up.

"Yeah baby," I said. "You want to meet up at my spot out south?"

"Yeah, send me the address and I'll head out that way now. It shouldn't take me that long since traffic has already died down," Red said.

"Bet," I responded then hung up the phone. I shot her a quick text with the address.

"Swear you just didn't say she hadn't been around your space like that? Bitch just said she was at your office," Memphis said with a suck of his teeth. He got up from his seat and headed towards the door. Stopping when he got to it, he turned around to face me. "Nigga you better hope Bleus get ahold of you before Falcon and I do. That nigga will just end you. But us?" He pointed to himself, then Falcon and Dove who sat staring at me. "We will make your ass suffer."

Chapter Seventeen

DOVE

I held on to the door handle as CJ turned the car. We were going so fast I was pretty sure we were on two wheels, but I knew better than to say anything to CJ 'cause he wasn't slowing down. We weren't waiting on Red to leave her mama's house, we were coming to her. And if Falcon and Memphis had anything to say about it, there wasn't a person in that house that was going to survive.

"Damn it, CJ, I'm going to throw up in this back seat if you don't slow the fuck down!" Bleus yelled over the music as he gripped the door closest to him. "Nigga, I know you trying to get there before she leave, but you driving too damn fast to not get us arrested before we even get there."

"Shit, my bad," CJ said. I felt the truck slow down as he took some of the pressure off the gas. "I'm just trying to get there before Falcon and Memphis crazy ass do. They just gonna start shooting as soon as they see her and I gotta find out if Benny is really in on this shit or not. "Look, I know Sage was your girl and all but I gotta know. Benny is like family to me and I gotta make sure before I do something I could regret later."

"I get it man, I really do," Bleus said with a nod. "For both y'all sake I hope that bitch just lucked up and started fucking with Benny and he wasn't a part of none of this shit."

"Umm baby," I said looking around at our surroundings confused.

"Yeah?" CJ said as he took another turn.

"Where are we going?" I questioned as I looked around.

"To Red's mama house," CJ said. He reached over and turned his music down so we could talk without having to yell.

"This ain't the way to Red's mama house," I said turning to face him. "Her mama lives on the other side of town."

"You sure, baby?" CJ said as he reached over into the cup holder and grabbed his phone.

"Yeah, her mama house is the one you picked me up from that time you got into with Tika. I don't know whose house this is, but it's definitely not her mama's."

"Could it be some of her people spot?" CJ questioned. I shook my head and turned back to look out the window. We parked about four houses down from where she was at and waited. A few seconds later the sound of his ringing phone was playing through the speakers. "Hello?"

"Aye man, cut your lights. That bitch in the car with some nigga in her driveway," Memphis said. He drove his car past the house Red was at and parked across from us.

"Memphis, how y'all get this location on Red?" CJ questioned as he cut his lights off.

"Benny had her drop her location so he could send her the address," Memphis said. I watched as he stepped out his car and run across the street to our car.

"This ain't her mama house," CJ said with a shake of his head after he rolled down the window.

"Shit, don't matter to me who house it is, I'm running up

on this bitch," Memphis said with a shrug of his shoulders. "Whoever she with about to get got, too."

Memphis tapped the door two times and took off towards the house with Falcon, Mickey, and Golden right behind him.

"Nigga nuttier than Falcon, I swear," CJ mumbled to himself as he pulled off his seatbelt and got out the car. I didn't even think twice as I got out the car and followed them.

"Nah, he riding for his people. I can't be mad at that," Bleus said as he jogged past us with his gun already in his hand.

"Aye get out the car, bitch!" I heard Memphis yell before dragging a screaming Red out the car by her hair. Falcon and Mickey stood by the driver door with their guns pointed at whoever was in the seat. "Shut up, damn girl," Memphis said as he put his gun to Red's temple, which immediately stopped her crying. "Yeah, I thought so. Pull that nigga out the car, too." Mickey nodded his head and pulled the driver door open. I damn near fell out when Detective Holmes stepped out the car with his pants hanging half off and his hands in the air.

"You gotta be fucking kidding me," CJ said with a laugh as he leaned against the car. "Nigga, you fucking with her ass?"

"You know who this nigga is?" Memphis asked. "You know what? That shit don't even matter. Let's get this inside before someone sees us."

"I'm not letting you into my house," Detective Holmes said.

"You don't have to nigga," Mickey said as he reached into the car and pulled out a set of keys. "We got the keys."

He tossed them to Falcon who only laughed and made her way to the house.

Chapter Eighteen

CJ

"Nigga, you weak as shit. I didn't even hit you that hard," Memphis said as he wiped his hand on Detective Holmes' shirt. They'd been at this for nearly two hours. One would ask questions and when Detective Holmes wouldn't give them the answer they wanted to hear, then they would take turns beating him.

"Well, you've been at it for so long that maybe those bitch ass hits you've been throwing are starting to hurt," Bleus said as he ate a sandwich. These fools had made themselves at home, making sandwiches and watching TV as they beat on Holmes and Red sat tied up in another room. I could hear her crying, but she wasn't loud enough to cause anyone to come looking.

"You want a go at him?" Memphis asked. "'Cause the entire time we been here, you been snacking and chilling like you at home."

"Shit, you said you had it under control," Bleus replied with a shoulder shrug and popped a grape in his mouth. I could tell from the way he was watching the room that Bleus was anything but calm. He was eating to keep himself occupied because every time he stopped eating, he would start pacing or start playing with his gun. Nigga was ready to snap, and I didn't blame him. We weren't getting the answers that we were looking for.

"Fuck it, y'all starting to get on my nerves," Golden said, brushing past Memphis and heading to the room that Red was tied up in. She came back out with a struggling Red. She pushed her in the chair next to Holmes and ripped the tape off her mouth. "I know that man already told you to stop all that crying. You starting to give me a headache. Now answer these fools' questions so I can go home and go to sleep. I'm tired."

"I ain't tellin' y'all shit. You'll have to kill me first," Red said looking over at all of us as if she was the one with the upper hand. Her eyes kept going back to Golden as if she was trying to figure out where she knew her from. Memphis laughed a little as he sat his food down and without wasting any time, he backhanded Red so hard she fell backwards in her seat.

"Contrary to popular belief, I don't like hitting women. But for you, I will make an exception," Memphis said as he stood over Red. "All I want to know is why you killed my sister."

"Nigga, fuck you," Red said as Memphis sat her chair upright. She tried and failed to smooth her hair down as she mugged Memphis up and down. "I don't even know you, so whatever questions you got for me don't mean shit."

"You ain't gotta know me, baby," Memphis said. He pulled a blunt out his pocket and lit it, never taking his eyes off Red as he did so. "But what you about to do is answer these questions I got."

"Or what, nigga?" Red asked with a smirk on her face.

"Or, baby girl," Memphis said, moving quickly towards her and grabbing her by the neck. "I'm going to beat your ass, drag you out this here house, drug you up, ship you down south and pimp your ass out until I'm tired of hearing you scream. I know about twenty different niggas that will gladly break your ass in before I toss you out in the streets and make a few dollars off you. And trust me when I tell you this, I learned this pimp shit from one of the best niggas in the game." Memphis took another pull of his blunt then blew the smoke into Red's face causing her to cough as he let her go. "Now are you gonna tell me what I need to know? Or are you going to keep playing games with me and I lose my patience with your ass."

"What do you want to know?" Red said.

"Who killed my sister?" Memphis questioned. He walked over to the corner of the room and grabbed a chair from the wall.

"If I don't know you, then I definitely don't know your sister," Red said shaking her head.

"Nah, you know my sister, baby girl. In fact, you know them all," Memphis said as he sat down in his chair.

"Who is your sister?" Red questioned.

"Falcon, Dove, Sage, Lilly and even Golden since I been rocking with her ass for too many years to count now," Memphis said as he pointed to each woman. Red quickly turned to where he was pointing to and let out a loud laugh.

"Nigga, you the brother Dove always said was a killer?" Red said. "Shit you might as well kill me now 'cause ain't shit I can do to save my life anyway." I didn't miss the way Red's eyes stayed on Dove. There was so much hate in her eyes that I wondered how there was ever a friendship. Just as quickly her eyes found Golden again, Red tilted her head to the side and watched her for a few seconds before she smiled.

"Tell me what I want to know, and I'll be nice and make sure your people can have an open casket," Memphis said.

Red brought her attention back to Memphis as she smacked her teeth in frustration.

"Shit, give me a cigarette, then," Red said with a shrug of her shoulders as she crossed her legs. It was like, just that fast she accepted her fate and came to terms with the fact she was going to die in this room and there was no escaping it. Memphis handed her a cigarette and lit it then threw the pack and the lighter on the table near her. Red took a pull of it and blew it out her mouth. "Alright so look, a few years ago Tika came to me with a fast money scheme. Somehow he hooked up with Mister through Holmes over there." She nodded her head towards Detective Holmes who was falling in and out of consciousness. "Mister put a hundred K on each one of all heads." Red shrugged her shoulders and took another pull of her cigarette then let out a small laugh as she blew the smoke out. "Tika was the only one dumb enough to volunteer for the shit, but at the last minute he changed his mind. He was looking to make some money for the long haul 'cause we was trying to get the fuck up out of here."

"Wait, so you and Tika was fucking around this entire time?" Falcon asked from her spot next to Dove. I'd figured they'd been fucking around for a while. The stories Dove used to tell me about them made it obvious. Maybe it was because I was on the outside looking in or because I'd seen niggas do that shit to females. Dove never thought so and because I didn't want to argue with her about it, I didn't bring it up.

"Up until the day he died. Shit, I even gave birth to his son a few months ago," Red said. She turned to look over at the girls, then brought her attention back to Memphis and Golden. "Baby girl, I've seen your face somewhere before haven't I?

"Don't worry about my face, tell these niggas what they want to know," Golden replied.

"So, what changed?" Bleus asked. He wanted answers and if Red was smart, she would keep spilling the secrets before one of our patience ran out.

"I don't know really 'cause the plan that Mister and Tika agreed on was simple. I would befriend Dove, watch her to make sure Rose hadn't started running her mouth and then report back. That's what we did for a few years, and monthly Mister would drop us eight grand for the information. Even if there wasn't anything new to tell, he still sent the money."

"Tika started catching feelings is what happened," I said. Red cut her eyes at me, but knew better to than say anything smart to me. Rolling her eyes at my comment, she continued to talk but there were only two things I was worried about: Dove's safety and Benny's part in all this. The rest of the shit didn't matter. There was something telling me that Benny's loyalty would still be in question if Red didn't stay on track.

"Anyway, after Tika proposed, Mister sent word that he wanted her taken out. Some shit about sending word to his connect to make it seem like an accident. I think it was really a sign to Rose to show her that he was still out there and could control some shit. Crazy thing was, he wasn't controlling shit 'cause each time he tried to set-up something, the shit fell through." Red let out a laugh and shook her head. "Plus, that was around the same time Tika got caught cheating and Dove called off the wedding and ended things with him. That made Tika snap. I'm talking about he called Mister demanding more money or he was going to tell it all. Mister told him to do it 'cause he wasn't afraid of shit." Red nodded and lit another cigarette "I have to give it to that nigga Mister, he wasn't backing down from shit. Him and Tika went at it for almost a damn year. Then she started fucking with CJ, and they both snapped."

"Why? He hadn't met CJ before," Memphis questioned.

"That's where I know you from!" Red said out the blue as

she turned to look at Golden. "You was that little stud bitch that started hanging out with Tika and the boys right before he went missing!" Red pointed at Golden and laughed. "Bitch, your ass was riding around with my nigga! Why the fuck am I the only one sitting here? That bitch needs to be right here next to me!"

"Girl if you don't pay the fuck attention!" Memphis roared as he snatched Red by her hair and pulled her to face him. "I'm only going to tell you one mo' time! Do what the fuck I'm telling you to do!"

"'Cause CJ name kept popping up because of Holmes over there," Red stammered as she pointed to Holmes who was out cold. Her eyes were damn near about to pop out her head as she did what Memphis told her to do. He dropped back down in her chair and retook his seat. "I guess they had some beef from back in the day and Holmes been trying to CJ caught up for years. But that shit never stuck, either. Shit, then Tika disappeared."

"He's dead," I said, interrupting her.

"Yeah, I figured you killed him," Red said, looking over at me. Her eyes watered with tears, but she never let them fall. She still loved that nigga. Even though he did her dirty, she was still holding him down.

"Nah baby girl, I didn't put that bullet in him," I said. Red eyed me for a second like she was trying to figure out if I was telling the truth before her eyes swung to Memphis, who shook his head no. Slowly Red's eyes bounced around the room to each person, who all shook their heads no, until they landed on Dove. Dove smiled brightly at Red and nodded her head. Memphis cleared his throat, bringing Red's attention back to him and the gun he slowly pulled from his waist.

"Where was I?" Red said as she wiped tears that she could no longer keep at bay. "Oh yeah, Holmes got involved more since Tika was gone. Like I said, we figured you killed him, so we were trying to either figure out how or where his body was."

"So y'all shot up the BBQ on some revenge type of shit?" Memphis asked.

"Pretty much. Shit, I was trying to get some quick cash 'cause Mister stopped paying a few weeks ago. He said something about not paying us another dime until somebody was dead, it didn't matter who it was. Holmes called me up and said he knew y'all was having a get-together and it would be the best time to take somebody out. I drove in the same night. We planned that shit out, stole a car, took a few guns out of inventory that Holmes said wouldn't be missed, and rolled out."

"You knew Sage was dead when you called me," Dove said with a shake of her head.

"Of course I knew, who you think took the shot?" Red said with a laugh. I jumped up just in time to stop Bleus from smashing her head in.

"Nah man, we got some more questions before you have your turn," I said to Bleus as I pushed him back. "Come on, if we gonna do this shit, let's get all of it out before you kill her."

"What else you wanna know? I just told you who killed Sage," Red said as she dropped her cigarette down on the ground and smashed it.

"Who else was helping you?" I asked.

"Oh, you wanna know if big dick Benny was supplying me with info, too?" Red said with another laugh. She glanced over at Lily to see if her words got under her skin, but all did Lily did was shrug her shoulders at her comment. "Nah, Benny was just an innocent by stander. Don't get me wrong, at first I was going to let that nigga take the blame for it all, but I decided to change my mind."

"Why?" Trigga asked. I pulled my phone from my pocket

and text Benny letting his know he could get out the car and come inside. He'd followed us here and had been waiting outside for my signal. I knew he was innocent, and his actions tonight proved it. There was no way a guilty man would be waiting for word on his innocence. If he had anything to do with any of this shit, he would've rolled out the first chance he got.

"Why what?" Red questioned. Benny walked in through the back and sat down next to me without saying a word.

"Why drag him into this shit," I said, instead of Trigga. "Why get caught up in some shit that aint have nothing to do with you? Why let that nigga have you stepping out of character? Shit, pick something out this story and ask why the fuck you have to be linked to this?"

"'Cause my nigga asked me to ride for him is why!" Red said with an attitude. "Tika and I were the real deal! Shit, after a while I was caught up in the shit and had to see it through. Like I said, I gotta a baby to take care of now. Hell, I still look after Tika daughter too, even though he gone. All I know is how to hustle and this shit was a quick come up."

"So, you was gonna take me out with you 'cause you dumb enough to ride for a nigga that wasn't really riding for you," Benny said with a shake of his head. He dropped his head and rubbed his hand over the top of it. "Shit is crazy to me, it don't make no sense. Yo' loyalty is to a nigga that wasn't loyal to you. He still chose Dove over you until the very end and you over here talking about y'all was the real deal."

"'Cause I've already come to terms with that fact I'm going to die. I'm ready to be with my man. I don't want to hear no damn lecture from nobody in this damn room," Red said. She straightened up in her seat and looked around, ready for whatever was about to come her way. "If y'all gonna kill me, y'all might as well do it, 'cause that's it. This shit was just for money. Tika went after Dove for a bag." Red pointed over at Holmes who was starting to come to again. “He was mad ‘cause you clowned his ass back in the day and couldn’t move past that shit. And y’all daddy just hated y’all. Nothing more to it.”

“That shit was personal for you, though,” Memphis said with a shake of his head as he got up from his seat. “Yo’ nigga fell for my sister and treated you like the side chick you always were. So, you wanted to prove you was better than her by jumping into this shit. Thinking you had the upper hand the entire time, when really you was just a pawn in Mister’s bullshit.” Red shrugged her shoulders, but didn’t verbally respond to what Memphis said.

“Baby you a sad ass bitch and you gonna follow that nigga to the grave for that shit,” Bleus said standing from his seat with his glock in his hand.

“At least I can stand by mine,” Red replied. She crossed her arms over her chest and waited. “That nigga Mister ain’t gonna stop. and yeah, y’all getting rid of me, but he gonna keep coming ‘cause he hates y’all more than I do.”

“Why?” I asked.

“I don’t know! Ask that nigga!” Red yelled.

“That nigga on my list, don’t worry. I already got eyes on him,” Memphis said.

“Then fucking kill me already!” Red replied. “I’m ready to see my man anyway.”

Bam!

Before she could say anything, Bleus put a bullet into her temple and her body dropped to the floor. If anyone was going to end Red’s life, it was going to be him. She’d taken Sage from him it was only right.

“What about this nigga?” Trigga said pointing to Holmes.

“Kill that nigga and make it look like a murder-suicide. He killed Red and then himself. We already found the drugs and guns, let this nigga people know he dirty,” I said as I pulled my phone out my pocket and dialed a number putting it on speaker phone. "Aye man, yo' partner is about to be out the game."

"Fuck that nigga, I got about three cases linked to him anyway. Shit I might drop some of my shit on him," Peters said with a laugh. "Make sure y'all clean the place up so when we sweep it, we never know it was y'all."

"Already on it, yo' brother got a few people waiting on his call to come in," I said looked over at Mickey who nodded his head and pulled out his on phone.

"Bet," Peters said then ended the call.

"Peters white ass works for you, too?" Holmes weakly asked. The loud bang of Bleus' gun had woken him up. "I should've known his ass wasn't shit. Fucking piece of shit."

"Peters been working for me longer than you been on my tail. Thanks to his big brother over there, I always knew your ass had it in for me. Why you think none of your cases stuck?" I said as I stood over him. "And just so you know, Peters ain't white. Nigga just look it. If you would've tried to get to know that nigga, you would've known that. He may have been raised by a white woman, but that's one hood grimy ass nigga."

"Fuck you CJ, I hope you rot in hell," Holmes said looking at me.

"Save me a seat," I said pulling out my gun and putting it under his chin. "Since you'll be there first." I pulled the trigger, blowing his brains out, ending this shit for good.

We didn't waste any time leaving since Mickey already had his people on the way to clean everything up. I stood outside the car, watching as Trigga and Golden argued outside my club. He wanted her to go with him and she had other plans. Trigga had been chasing behind Golden since the night we snatched up Tika. The fact that she was linked to Memphis this entire time only made me laugh. Falcon rested her head on Mickey's shoulder as they leaned against the hood of their car. Every so often, the gun that she had in her hand would glimmer from the streetlight as she tapped it against her leg. Bleus sat against his car with tears running down his face. I knew to let him mourn his own way. From the moment Sage died, he hadn't taken the time to grieve her properly. Since finding the reason for her death, the tears hadn't stopped flowing for him. Memphis stood next to him, giving him silent support with his own tears falling.

"Baby, I'm ready to go," Dove said as she put her hand into mine. "I want to shower, lay down, and just sleep."

"Okay mama, we can go," I said nodding at her. I pulled her closer to me and unlocked the truck doors, helping her into the truck without another word. I said my goodbyes to everyone, then climbed into the truck.

I pulled off with Dove in the passenger seat, allowing her to work over her emotions just like Bleus was doing. The second Blues pulled the trigger, he closed a chapter for all of us. They now had the answers for Sage's death and even some type of closure. Memphis already had a plan in motion for Mister and said he would be putting him in the ground shortly. Mister was one twisted ass nigga for putting money on his kids' heads. I reached over and palmed Dove's stomach with one hand as I drove. Even though the baby wasn't here yet, I would give him or her the world before I even thought about taking them out of it.

"What about Benny?" Dove said as she wiped her tears away. I reached over and tapped the screen on my dash. Pulling up my call log, I hit Benny's number.

"Yeah?" Benny answered.

"I wanted to just check in with you," I said as I stopped at a red light. "I know tonight was stressful and I needed to see where your head was at. We ain't ever questioned each other loyalty before. I should've known better than to start questioning yours tonight."

"Don't trip off it, bro," Benny said. "If the shoes were on the other foot, I would be questioning shit too. I appreciate you not putting a bullet in my head before finding out the truth first."

"Never that," I said with a small laugh. "Aye, but check this shit out. She was working with Holmes the entire time. That nigga Mister got so many people in his pocket." I explained to Benny, since he wasn't in the room when Red started running her mouth.

"You should've put a bullet in Holmes weak ass a long time ago," Benny said with a laugh of his own. "I told you back in the day you shouldn't have fucked with his sister like that, but you just had to get head from that bitch."

"Shit, now I know nigga," I said as I pulled into the driveway. "But I don't think this shit is over with."

"What you mean?" Benny questioned.

"Red said Mister is gonna keep coming at them. I believe her ass. That nigga hate his own seeds with a passion," I replied.

"So, what's the next move?" Benny said. The way he said it let me know he was down for whatever and would have my back. Shit hit me hard 'cause for a second I questioned my nigga's loyalty, and I knew better than that.

"Shit, for now I'm going to take care of my woman and have her back. Memphis already said he was on the lookout for Mister and it don't look like he gonna leave no time soon. So I'm going to let that nigga handle it. He wants his redemption so damn bad, then he can get it by taking out they pops," I replied as I brushed my hands over my head. "But shit let me get Dove into the house, I'll holla at you tomorrow."

"Bet," Benny replied then hung up.

I shut the truck off and looked over at Dove, only to

realize that she'd fallen asleep. I jumped out the truck and quickly got to her side. I didn't even wake her as I pulled her out, took her in the house, and put her in the bed. After showering, I climbed in, pulled her close, and fell asleep. For the first time in a long time, I slept peacefully. Knowing that I'd finally taken care of the pain that haunted Dove for the last few months.

EPILOGUE

Dove

1 year later...

"You try and push out a damn baby and then tell me it's not that bad," I yelled as I stormed through the house, CJ on my heels trying to calm me down, as I moved like I was on the biggest warpath in history.

"Dove, I said I would help!" CJ fussed as I pushed open the doors to his office. Benny, Mickey, Trigga, and Memphis sat around trying not to laugh as I stormed over to his desk and waited.

"How the hell are you going to help, CJ? Peyton and Xavier are only seven months old!" I said as I swiped papers off his desk and searched. "We don't have time for ourselves now and you want to add more kids? Like what kind of nigga are you to want to add to this madness?"

"It's simple," CJ said with a laugh as he walked into the office with our boys in his arms. "Falcon and Mickey's baby is going to need someone to hang out with. Peyton and Xavier have Juke, its only right that baby Scavenger has someone close to his or her age to play with."

"Nigga, if you don't stop calling my child Baby Scavenger, I swear I'm going to let my wife shoot you," Mickey said with a laugh.

"Pick a damn name so I know what to call it, then!" CJ said as he sat the boys down to crawl around the room. "And what the hell are you looking for?"

"My car keys," Dove said and rolled her eyes. "I'm supposed to meet Falcon and Lily at Carters for lunch, and I can't find my keys. The last place I saw them was in here."

"Your keys are by the door where I put them this morning after I came back from filling up your tank," CJ said with a shake of his head.

I looked up at him and smiled because I wasn't really looking for my keys, but I couldn't let him know that. Falcon called me while he was at the gas station earlier and told me she overheard Mickey and CJ talking this morning about a ring and after popping out two kids and him wanting another I definitely wasn't about to pop out another kid without a ring on my finger.

"Shit, you're right," I said moving towards him. I stopped and kissed the boys who were playing in the floor before kissing him goodbye and leaving.

CJ

I pushed inside of Dove faster than she expected, making her moan even louder as I started to pound away at her. The minute she walked into the house, I had a hard dick and was horny as hell. I knew I was about to fuck the shit out of her. She looked good as hell in a pair of high waisted jeans, a grey sheer top, and a pair of wedge heels. It was something about her confidence after she had the boys that kept my dick hard. She embraced her looks and wore that shit like a badge of honor. And, as her nigga, I wanted to make sure she knew how much I loved that shit.

"Shit CJ, slow down," Dove moaned. She reached back and tried to push me away, but I wasn't having that.

"Nah, fuck all that," I said as I smacked her ass. "When I told you to slow down 'cause I was about to nut, what did you do, huh?" I smacked her ass again and pushed deeper inside her. She tried to crawl away, but I'd chained her ankles to the bed post, so she wasn't going anywhere.

"I'm sorry!" she screamed. But I knew she wasn't 'cause she was bouncing her ass on my dick. Her ass wasn't sorry for shit and we both knew it.

"You have no idea how sorry your ass is about to be," I said as I sped up. I was hitting her squishy spot that only I could reach, which was causing her pussy to grip my dick so tight that I could feel my nut starting to form again. "You gonna give me another baby, Dove?"

"CJ," Dove whined.

"It's a simple yes or no, Dove," I told her. I started to rotate my hips, which hit a different spot. "You gonna give me another baby?"

"Ohh CJ," Dove moaned. "I'm about to cum, baby."

"You ain't cumming till you answer my question," I said as I stopped moving and reached around her to pinch her clit. "I swear I'll pull out and not let you cum if you don't answer me."

"CJ, stop playing," Dove whined as she tried to move back and forth on my dick. I leaned forward putting my weight on her to keep her from moving. "Stop playing, CJ!"

"I ain't playing, mama," I said in between kissing the side of her face. "I want you to give me another baby. Can you do that for me?" I started moving again. This time slowly working her pussy. Dove loved sex rough and hard, but when I went slow and worked her body she responded more. I learned to ask the questions that I wanted to know the answers to by working her body this way. "Come on Dove, have another one of my babies," I whispered into her ear before gently biting it. "Please baby, give me a daughter this time."

"Okay CJ," Dove moaned. I kept my slow pace, feeling her orgasm build up. Her pussy gripped my dick so tight that I knew that we weren't going to last too much longer. "Shit! I'm cumming." Just as she finished her sentence, I felt her squirt on my dick which was my signal that I could follow her.

"I'm pretty sure I got you pregnant with that load," I said with a laugh as I pulled out of her. I unbuckled Dove's ankles and helped her out the bed. Without responding, Dove made her way to the bathroom and slammed the door shut. I walked over to the dresser. Laughing, I searched through the bottom drawer and pulled out the ring I had stashed in a pair of rolled up socks. Whistling, I made my way to the bathroom, where Dove was already in the shower.

"Aye, what's your problem?" I said as I knocked on the clear shower door.

"Nothing CJ," Dove said without looking at me as she washed her body.

"Then why you acting like that?" I said with a laugh.

"Like what?" Dove said.

"Like I didn't just give you some bomb ass head and stroke your insides until you squirted all over my shit?" I said as I pulled the shower door open. "What I do to piss you off?" I put the ring on my pinky so I wouldn't drop it. Even though I had a big ass dinner scheduled for a few days from now where I planned to propose, something inside me made me want to do it now.

"It's fine CJ, I just want to shower and then go to sleep. The boys will be back in the morning from my mama and Chester's, and I want to get some sleep before they do," Dove said as she stepped into the water, letting the water run down the front of her body.

"Alright," I said. "Hand me your loofa and I'll wash you back." I dropped down to my knee.

"Here," Dove huffed as she reached behind her to hand me the loofa. "CJ, here is the loofa." She twisted the loofa from side-to-side before finally turning around. Her eyes dropped down to me and her face twisted in confusion. "What are you doing?"

"About to wash your legs, hand me the loofa," I said with a smile. She handed it to me, and I started to wash her feet, working my way up her leg. Never taking my eyes off hers, I watched her as she watched me. "I love you, Dove."

"I love you too, Clever," Dove said with a soft smile. I finished washing her body then she washed me. Her eyes damn near bucking out her head when she saw the ring on my finger. "CJ, what's this?" She raised my hand to get a better look at the three-carat, vintage three-stone, emerald-cut diamond ring that her mama and sister helped me pick out.

"Oh, that's your engagement ring if you say you want to be my wife," I said. I pulled the ring off my finger and took her hand in mine. "I know I talk about a lot shit, but it ain't nothing else in the world that I would rather have you do than to become my wife."

"Yes!" Dove said with a smile as she wrapped her arms around me.

"Damn girl, I couldn't even ask you the question," I said

with a laugh as I pulled her arms from around my neck. "Dove Lincoln, will you marry me?"

"Hell yeah!" Dove said with her own laugh as I put the ring on her finger. After I was done, she pulled my face to hers and kissed me. Reaching down I lifted her up and pinned her against the wall. "CJ," she said, pulling away from our kiss.

"Yeah baby?" I said as I lined my hard dick up to the opening of her pussy.

"You getting your way too, 'cause I'm already pregnant," Dove moaned as I slid into her. I laughed as I started to move in and out of her, careful to not to slip on the wet floor.

The End

WANT TO BE A PART OF THE GRAND PENZ FAMILY?

To submit your manuscript to Grand Penz Publications,
please send the first three chapters and synopsis to
grandpenzpublications@gmail.com

www.ingramcontent.com/pod-product-compliance
Ingram Content Group UK Ltd.
Pitfield, Milton Keynes, MK11 3LW, UK
UKHW041852190726
13854UKWH00002B/862